HIS HIGHLAND LASS

THE CLAN SINCLAIR BOOK ONE

CELESTE BARCLAY

OLIVER HEBER BOOKS

All rights reserved.

No part of this publication may be sold, copied, distributed, reproduced or transmitted in any form or by any means, mechanical or digital, including photocopying and recording or by any information storage and retrieval system without the prior written permission of both the publisher, Oliver Heber Books and the author, Celeste Barclay, except in the case of brief quotations embodied in critical articles and reviews.

PUBLISHER'S NOTE: This is a work of fiction. Names, characters, places, and incidents either are the product of the author's imagination or are used fictitiously. Any resemblance to actual persons, living or dead, business establishments, events, or locales is entirely coincidental.

Copyright © 2018 by Celeste Barclay.

0 9 8 7 6 5 4 3 2 1

Published by Oliver Heber Books

❦ Created with Vellum

This little story is my first endeavor as a historical romance author. I'm thankful to all the historical romance authors I read who inspired me to free my imagination.

Happy reading y'all,
Celeste

SUBSCRIBE TO CELESTE'S NEWSLETTER

Subscribe to Celeste's bimonthly newsletter to receive exclusive insider perks.

Subscribe Now

THE CLAN SINCLAIR

His Highland Lass
His Bonnie Highland Temptation
His Highland Prize
His Highland Pledge
His Highland Surprise
Their Highland Beginning

SINCLAIR FAMILY TREE

Liam Sinclair m. Kyla Sutherland

b. Callum Sinclair m. Siùsan Mackenzie (SH-IY-oo-san)
  b. Thormud Seamus Magnus Sinclair (TOR-mood SHAY-mus)
  b. Rose Kyla Sinclair

b. Alexander Sinclair m. Brighde Kerr (BREE-ju KAIR)

b. Tavish Sinclair m. Ceit Comyn (KAIT-ch CUM-in)

b. Magnus Sinclair m. Deidre Fraser (DEER-dreh FRA-zer)

b. Mairghread Sinclair m. Tristan Mackay (Mah-GAID)
  b. "Wee" Liam Brodie Mackay

CHAPTER 1

She entered the Great Hall like a strong spring storm in the northern most Highlands. Tristan Mackay felt like it blew him hither and yon. As the storm settled, she left him with the sweet scents of heather and lavender wafting toward him as she approached. She wasn't a classic beauty, tall and willowy like the women at court. Her face and form weren't what legends were made of. But she held a unique appeal unlike any he'd seen before. His eyes riveted to her long chestnut hair with strands of fire and burnt copper running through them. Unlike the waves or curls he was used to, her hair was unusually straight and fine, a waterfall cascading down her back. While she wasn't tall, neither was she short. She had a figure meant for a man to grasp and hold onto, whether from the front or from behind. She had an aura of confidence and charm, but not arrogance or conceit, like many good-looking women of his acquaintance. She didn't seem to realize her own appeal. Intuition told him she was many things, but one thing she wasn't was his.

Mairghread Sinclair was intended for his brother—his

*step*brother, Alan. She and her father, Liam, and her four brothers approached with a contingent of guardsmen behind them. They had left even more guardsmen in the inner bailey, attending to their horses. The Mackays and Sinclairs hadn't been on good terms of late, and an alliance between Tristan's stepbrother and the Sinclair's daughter created a truce between the two raiding clans. Within the last three years, both sides burned numerous crofts and fields, and countless heads of cattle and sheep switched back and forth between the two. However, when an out-and-out clash between raiders, who met coincidentally, one night left fifteen Sinclairs dead and eighteen Mackays dead or wounded, both chiefs decided they needed a truce. The strongest way to secure that and to form an alliance was through marriage. As there were no eligible females in the Mackay laird's family to marry off to one of the Sinclair brothers, it fell to Mairghread to marry a Mackay. Tristan didn't consider himself ready, or even inclined, to marry at this point. He suspected his stepbrother, Alan, would benefit from settling down and sowing his seed in only one woman, rather than any who allowed him to get his meaty hands onto them long enough to lift his plaid. A quick pang of guilt flashed through his mind as he sensed Mairghread was the sacrificial lamb.

Tristan stepped down from the dais where he had been eating his midday meal with his stepbrother and stepmother, Lady Beatris. As the Sinclair party approached, he observed a wary expression cross each of their faces as they looked past Tristan to where Alan and Beatris remained seated. He almost groaned at their rudeness. This wasn't the first impression he hoped to make. He didn't dare glance back, since he didn't want to make their rudeness any more obvious than it already was.

When Tristan reached Laird Sinclair, he reached out his arm to grasp the other chief's forearm in greeting. He noted Liam Sinclair was a bear of a man. He was barrel chested and stood almost as tall as Tristan's six and a half feet. While he had to be at least fifty years old, if he was a day, his hair and beard were still the same dark chestnut as his daughter. In fact, all Liam's children shared his coloring, but while the men had brown eyes, his daughter had a blue-gray unlike any shade he'd seen before.

When he turned to greet Mairghread, she took his breath away once more. She had unblemished skin, slightly darkened from time in the sun. There was a hint of freckles across the bridge of her nose and across the tops of her cheekbones. Her nose was neither narrow nor pointy, like most women he knew. It had a soft, almost flat, finish to the tip. He was sure her profile would be gentle and rounded rather than harsh and angular. Her lips drew his attention away from her eyes and nose. They were a perfect bow shape and pink, but almost closer to red. They looked soft and kissable. He almost shook his head to clear his thoughts. He had no business fantasizing about how those lips would feel against his. He ran a hand through his shoulder length, jet black hair.

"Welcome to Castle Varrich. On behalf of ma stepmother, stepbrother, and Clan Mackay, I welcome ye. I trust yer journey went smoothly." Tristan gathered his thoughts enough to say something to his guests.

"Thank ye for having us, Laird Mackay." Clearly, Liam wasn't a man of many words.

Tristan turned to Mairghread, hoping to be gracious. "Lady Mairghread, we have prepared a chamber for ye above stairs if ye would like to retire until the evening meal."

A flash of annoyance crossed Mairghread's face, but it disappeared as quickly as it came. She looked at Tristan and plastered what she hoped was a serene smile on her face. "Thank ye, Laird Mackay. I would like to refresh maself and have a moment to change out of ma travel clothes. However, I've been atop a horse for three days. I'd really like to stretch ma legs. Perhaps someone might show me the gardens." She looked pointedly over his shoulder at her soon-to-be betrothed.

Alan was still shoveling food into his mouth as though it would be his last meal for days. The Mackays knew Alan to indulge in all things, whether it was food, drink, or women. His mother only encouraged him, and he was as spoiled an adult as he had been a child. Fortunately for him and for the clan, he loved to train as much as he loved to imbibe in drink and women. It was the only way he kept himself from being as round as a barrel. He must have sensed several pairs of eyes on him, because he finally looked up.

Tristan turned to face the dais, as it was impossible to ignore any longer that neither his stepbrother nor his stepmother came forward to greet their guests. It took quite a great deal to embarrass Tristan, but now he wasn't only embarrassed but ashamed of his family. Alan hadn't jumped at the idea of marrying, and certainly not a Sinclair, but he'd come around to the idea when he realized a wife meant a guaranteed woman to warm his bed each night.

"Lady Beatris, I'd ask ye kindly to show Lady Mairghread to her chamber, please. Then, Alan, mayhap ye'd take Lady Mairghread for a turn or two around the gardens. It might be a pleasant way to become acquainted with yer future *wife*." Tristan turned back to notice the Sinclair brothers glaring at Alan. Their future brother-by-marriage clearly failed to impress them.

Tristan watched as Lady Beatris led Mairghread, albeit grudgingly, up the stairs to her chamber. Alan came down from the dais for Tristan's introduction to his intended's family. Tristan surmised Liam was sizing Alan up, both physically and by his character. While Alan's clear warrior physique pleasantly impressed Liam, his lips turned down when he looked into

Alan's eyes. He glanced toward the stairs Beatris and Mairghread had just taken. An expression of regret flashed so quickly across his eyes that Tristan wasn't sure if he'd made it up in his own mind. When he looked to the other men, he noticed Mairghread's brothers had stealthily formed a slight semicircle around Alan. He was almost boxed in, with no way to move forward unless they let him pass.

Tristan listened as they each introduced themselves to Alan. The oldest and tánaiste, or heir, was Callum, and he seemed to be the calmest of the group. Alexander, who served at Callum's second, followed him. He had an air of authority that matched his brother's, but he seemed more shrewd and cunning. Tristan deduced he was one with whom to be careful not to make an enemy. The third brother, Tavish, was the shortest of the four, but only by a hair. He most resembled their father in build. While the other three brothers were broad across the chest and shoulders, Tavish had their father's barrel chest. The fourth and youngest brother, Magnus, was the largest of the lot. He looked as though he tossed cabers as a daily warm up before training for eight hours. He looked like a positive giant. Tristan was aware Magnus and Mairghread were the closest in age and were extremely close. For Alan's sake, he hoped Alan never angered Magnus, as Tristan wasn't certain Alan would survive.

Tristan picked up the conversation as Alan remembered his manners. He caught Alan saying, "Mayhap ye would like to join our men out in the training yard. I would join ye, but as ye heard, I must take yer sister out for a walk." Perhaps he had not remembered his manners after all.

Tristan almost cringed at Alan's tone. He made it sound like he was being forced to take a dog out for a walk rather than spend time with his future wife. While all the Sinclair men's faces remained neutral, there was a shift in the air. Things weren't off to a good start. Not good in the least. Tristan only hoped the afternoon would turn the situation around. Or they might never get around to signing the betrothal papers.

In her chambers, Mairghread breathed a calming breath as she turned to face her soon-to-be mother-by-marriage. Just the walk to the chamber had been enough to grate on Mairghread's nerves. Lady Beatris had a whining lilt to her already nasal voice. She hadn't come up for air once she launched into describing all the wonderful attributes her son possessed. While the woman was convinced of every single word she spoke, it sounded as if she were a tinker selling her son, and he were a shiny trinket made from dinged and warped iron.

When Lady Beatris paused to close the door, Mairghread found her opportunity to speak up. "Lady Beatris, thank ye for showing me the way. I shall only be a moment while I change. I notice ma trunk has already made its way up here. I will return to the Great Hall to join yer son on our walk."

While that was as strong a hint as Mairghread dared give, she hoped the woman would take it. That wasn't the case. "Lady Mairghread, I'd be happy to help ye with yer gowns. Though I see ye dinna follow the court fashions." Beatris turned her nose up at Mairghread. "The well-polished and sophisticated ladies of the court wear the ties to their gowns in the back. It takes at least one lady-in-waiting or maid to assist them in and out of their gowns. Ye might consider a change in yer wardrobe once ye become the wife of the Clan Mackay tánaiste. A wardrobe that better suits yer elevated status, mayhap."

Mairghread gritted her teeth. Liam had presented her at court several times over the course of her life, as he was a well-respected Highland laird. She was all too aware of what happened at court, from the wardrobes of those women to their scheming and unchaste behavior. She had wanted no part of that in the past and wanted no part of it now. She preferred her gowns to have the ties in the front, so she didn't have to rely on anyone to assist her. She enjoyed her privacy—the little that she had with four brothers—and when she retired to her chamber, she liked to be alone. As for elevated status, she didn't see how this elevated her status in any way. She was the only daughter of one of the wealthiest and most powerful lairds in the Highlands, in all of Scotland. She was a wealthy heiress in her own rights, as her dowry included many household items, jewelry, and a passel of land. She loosened her jaw and forced herself to relax.

I have naught to prove to that auld biddy. She blathers on a bit. Does she ever haud her wheest?

"I dinna care for court fashion as I find it impractical for ma duties around the keep. I prefer to dress maself than have a maid do it. I like ma privacy." A stronger hint given.

Will she get it?

"Och, well, aye then. I shall meet ye below." Beatris left with a harrumph and a swish of her skirts.

Mairghread released the breath she hadn't realized she held. She slipped out of her kirtle and splashed water onto her face and neck. There was a drying cloth folded on the table next to the bowl, and she spotted her bar of lavender and heather soap on the other side. She made quick work of washing herself down as best as possible without a tub. She was into a new kirtle and on her way out of the chamber in less than five minutes.

I may as well get this walk over with. I wish I hadnae said aught. I might have gone by maself if I hadnae opened ma gob. That man is vile, and I will tie myself to him for the rest of ma life. Bluidy bleeding hell.

Her inner monologue ceased as she reached the bottom of the stairs and stepped into the Great Hall. She looked at her brothers and father and realized in the short time she was abovestairs, things hadn't improved. All four brothers stood with their arms crossed and appeared to be listening intently to whatever Alan was saying. However, after a lifetime of her father's mannerisms, which her brothers had adopted either by nature or nurture, she knew what their stance meant. They weren't pleased. They hid their disdain and boredom mostly, but their crossed arms showed they didn't welcome Alan into the conversation like they had Laird Mackay.

At the thought of Laird Mackay, her eyes shifted to search for him. He stood apart from the other men as he talked to someone she hadn't seen earlier. Both brothers were warriors in their build, but Laird Mackay was the brawest man she'd ever laid eyes on. As her mind settled on an image of green eyes, her curiosity demanded she get a closer peek at his. Were they emerald or more like moss after it rained? Her breath caught again, just as it had when she arrived, and her eyes adjusted to the dimness of the Great Hall after being outside. He was unlike any man she'd met in her two-and-twenty years. He was built like an oak tree with trunks for legs, ones that she peered at below his plaid and above his mid-calf boots. He had the arms of a blacksmith; his forearms had to be almost as wide around as her thigh. His shoulders were so broad it wouldn't surprise her if he turned sideways to go through most doorways, and he probably had to bend down as well. He had to be close to six and a half feet tall. She had always considered her brothers to be the most impressively built men she'd ever seen, but Tristan Mackay made them resemble lads who still had some growing to do. Even her giant of a brother, Magnus, didn't seem as braw as Tristan.

Mairghread forced her eyes away from Tristan. But as soon as they settled on Alan, she wished she hadn't. He was a disappointment in comparison. She knew she shouldn't view him that way, but it was the truth to her. While he had the physique of a well-trained warrior, he just didn't seem as braw as his stepbrother. He had fair hair and blue eyes, both nondescript shades. It was clear they came from different stock as they weren't blood relatives, but from what she understood, they'd grown up together from being weans.

There was an arrogance about Alan that Mairghread found exceedingly off putting. No one had noticed her enter the Great Hall yet, so she took the opportunity to observe her future betrothed. He still talked with her family, but from her current position, she noticed how his eyes darted around the Great Hall as though he were looking for something. When his gaze landed on a busty serving woman, and he smirked, Mairghread got an even better sense of the man they meant her to marry. She continued to watch Alan. He moved on to gaze at another two women in much the same way. One approached the group of men with a tray of ale for each. She leaned forward as she served her brothers, giving them an unobstructed view of her ample bosom. As she leaned forward, she positioned her backside next to Alan. He gave her a surreptitious pinch as he grinned at the Sinclairs. As she walked away, he gave her an overt pat on the backside. She was positive one of her brothers growled. Next, he looked at two much younger serving women. It was impossible that the young women were over sixteen or seventeen years old. They both took a step back from the table they were clearing. He frightened them, and they didn't want his attention.

So, he chases all the women employed in the keep. Or, at least, the ones he considers worth bedding. The aulder women enjoy his attention, but the younger ones shy away. I wonder if that's the case with most of them. What does he do that has the more experienced women showing him attention while the inexperienced want naught to do with him? Is he skilled in the bedchamber, or does he lavish his women with gifts or special privileges? Or have these women learned it's easier to do his bidding?

Once again, Mairghread found her mind running away with her as she assessed her potential husband. In her mind, he was moving away from definitively being her new husband to being only a potential husband. She was aware this wouldn't do her any good. She needed to accept what was already in the works. Whether or not she liked him wouldn't sway the need for an alliance or her father's mind. She fervently hoped she was only seeing a superficial version of Alan and that there would be more substance, even if it took time to find it. Perhaps he would improve once he committed to her and to marriage. Somehow, the back of her mind kept telling her that didn't seem likely.

She knew she couldn't hide much longer, or people would wonder what kept her. She didn't want the Mackays to get the idea she would be awkward and prim. Taking too long to reappear might give them the impression she was materialistic and fussy, so she stepped into the hall and walked toward the six men. As she walked past the woman Alan pinched, she didn't miss the enmity in the woman's eyes. She passed two more women who gave her much the same hostility. As she passed an older woman, she noticed pity. The two younger women who had cleaned the table also gave her looks of pity.

So those who ken him pity me, and those who ken *him find me to be competition.*

Mairghread offered warm smiles to all whom she passed. She said hello to those who seemed willing to hear her. Once she joined the men, they all turned to watch at her. It made her self-conscious to have all these eyes on her because she sensed everyone else in the hall was looking at her, too. Understandably, they were trying to gain any insight into the new lady in the keep. She turned her warmest smile on Alan and almost gasped at the leer he gave her. His eyes never traveled higher than her cleavage, which she had an ample amount showing since most summer gowns hid it poorly. Her aversion to walking in the gardens with him grew. She didn't want to be anywhere near him and certainly not alone, but she was the one who had mentioned it.

Alan extended his arm to her. "Shall we take that turn aboot the garden, ma sweet? I realize now it was an excellent suggestion. I only wish I'd come up with it maself." His candied words made her want to retreat. Her intuition screamed a warning about being around him. She couldn't put her finger on it. It wasn't pure fear or pure revulsion, but some combination of the two. She placed her hand on his forearm, but he tucked it around the crook of his arm and dragged her toward the door. She shot an anxious glance over her shoulder at Magnus, and the nod of her head was so brief Tristan almost missed it as he watched from where he spoke to his captain of the guard. Magnus immediately fell into step behind them. Alan turned back and glared at him, but Magnus simply crossed his arms and shrugged. Mairghread didn't understand how he walked with his arms crossed, but it certainly made him appear even fiercer than normal.

The trio made their way down the steps to the inner bailey. The keep was designed in three parts, with the original tower on the left closest to the gate, whereas the midsection of the keep was boxier with three stories. There were arrow slits on the second floor, and proper windows on the third. Mairghread's chamber was on the second floor and had two arrow slits. She assumed the laird's family chambers were on the third floor and enjoyed proper windows. The third section of the keep was the kitchens. As they turned in that direction, Mairghread waited for Alan to tell her about what they passed, but his attention was everywhere but on her.

Mairghread appreciated the respite from talking, as she had nothing to say to him. She looked at each of the buildings they passed. Just outside the kitchens were large ovens used to bake the day's bread. Tucked behind the kitchens, close to the bailey wall, was the laundry. She watched women working at a cauldron over a large fire. There were two women with large wooden spoons the length of a man stirring the contents while another five stood over a trough scraping clothes along washboards. The last thing she noticed were four more women moving along the clothes lines, taking down dry clothes and replacing them with the wet ones. It reminded her of home. She had often helped the women with the laundry. While they would never let her do any of the actual washing, she helped with the clothes lines.

Directly across from the laundry, the noise and heat coming from the blacksmith's forge reached her. The din was almost overwhelming. The blacksmith, and what looked to be three apprentices, was busy working on horseshoes and swords. The apprentices resembled the blacksmith, with a shocking blaze of carrot-orange hair.

Must be his sons.

Next came a series of small buildings with no one about. Mairghread assumed these were storage buildings, and most likely held seed, threshed wheat, shorn wool, and any other item of which there was an overabundance. Mairghread had noticed the stables when they came through the portcullis. She longed to check on her horse, Firelight. She would ask Alan on their way back.

Alan yanked on Mairghread's arm to draw her to the left. He pulled hard enough that she almost stumbled. Rather than slow down or apologize, he huffed and made a sound of impatience. Mairghread heard her brother growl from behind them. She sensed more than saw Magnus close the gap between them. If Alan halted, Magnus would plow into him. For a second, it tempted Mairghread to make that happen. However, she didn't want to antagonize Alan. She was unsure whether he had a temper. She got the distinct sense he was the type who did, so she kept moving.

They approached the gardens, and Alan opened the gate, but didn't wait for Mairghread to pass through first. In fact, the gate almost slammed shut on her. Magnus's arm shot forward to push the gate back open and let her pass through. She raised her eyebrows at her brother as she said thank you.

"Are ye coming, or just going to wait at the entrance? Ye said ye wanted to tour the gardens. Here they are." Alan's tone was anything but inviting. Mairghread was quickly running out of patience for all things Mackay, well, all things Mackay other than Tristan.

CHAPTER 2

*A*lan spent all of twenty minutes in Mairghread and Magnus's company once they entered the garden. He excused himself with a trite "I must check on the men." He skedaddled, moving as though his pants were on fire. The siblings wandered through the garden at a leisurely pace. They weren't even ten months apart in age and were more like twins than anything else. They had been constant companions from the time Mairghread crawled fast enough to catch up to a toddling Magnus. She was close to all her brothers, but she and Magnus were inseparable except for when they had to be, or Magnus gallivanted about with the other men. Mairghread was aware of what they got up to, as she had made the mistake of following Magnus when she was four-and-ten, and he was five-and-ten.

Mairghread got more of an eyeful than she had ever expected when she showed up at the back of the village alehouse. There was Magnus with his plaid thrown up to his shoulders, arse to the wind, thrusting into a barmaid. It shocked her so much, she hadn't made a sound for at least a good thirty seconds. Then she squeaked. She had never squeaked in her life, but she did then. Magnus whirled around to catch his sister, wide eyed and open-mouthed. He didn't know what to do. The top half of him wanted to run after his sister and apologize, of all things, but the bottom half of him wanted to finish what he'd started. At five-and-ten, it took him but a couple more minutes to finish what he was amid, then he dashed off after his sister without a word or a coin to the barmaid. He'd caught up to his sister and pulled her to a stop.

A conversation that neither had ever imagined they would have ensued. Magnus explained the mechanics to her. And much, much more. With no living mother to explain these things to Mairghread, and a father who would never, could never, have such a conversation with his daughter, the responsibility fell onto Magnus's young shoulders. Mairghread learned more about the goings on between a man and a woman than she ever imagined. While Magnus admitted he wasn't the most experienced, he had now done it enough times to give some insight. Magnus answered each and every question Mairghread had, and there were quite a lot. By the end, Mairghread understood there was more to coupling than just the breeding she'd seen between horses in the pastures and the cattle on the hills.

"Do ye suppose he's checking on his men, or did he have a wench to tup?" Mairghread wondered aloud.

"Yer intended seems to have quite a relationship with many of the women in this clan. There were at least two in the keep that he kens intimately. I noticed at least five more in various parts of the bailey who looked at him either with desire or revulsion. Both looks lead me to believe he kens them well."

They found a bench next to a rosebush and took a seat. Mairghread turned her face toward the sun. She'd never cared that too much sun brought out freckles. She believed the feeling of sun on her skin was one of the best she knew. She would soak up as much as she dared in the spring and summer months before losing the sun's rays for most of autumn and almost all of winter.

"I dinna suppose he will give up his women once we marry." This caused Mairghread a great deal of sadness. While she didn't believe she had to have a love match, she believed she should have a faithful husband. Even though she was aware many men were unfaithful to their wives, especially noblemen, the men within her clan didn't do that. A man who didn't keep the vow he made before God, his bride, and his clan was a man without honor. A man without honor was no real Highlander.

"Perhaps ye will win him over with yer beauty and knowledge." Magnus smirked down at her. While she had no firsthand carnal knowledge, she and Magnus carried on several conversations beyond the one in the village after the incident at the alehouse. Magnus had been open with her, as he wanted to prepare her for whatever might be in store for her. He wanted no one to take advantage of his sister, and he wished her a happy marriage. A happy marriage bed was part of a happy marriage, or so the married guardsman had told him.

"I dinna think that will be enough for him to change his ways. I would hazard a guess he doesnae realize his ways could use a change. And if he does, I dinna think he wants to."

"Ye may vera well be right aboot that. Can ye come to live with that?" Magnus's concern rang in his tone.

"Do I have any choice?"

"Nay, I suppose ye dinna. Do ye imagine ye will find happiness here, anyway?" Magnus wrapped his arm around Mairghread's shoulder, and she leaned into him. She always found great comfort in hugs from her father and brothers. Perhaps it was because they were so much larger than her. It always gave her an immediate sense of security and belonging when they wrapped their powerful arms around her. This time was no different. She realized with a pang how she would miss this once she married, and they left. What comfort would she find in her new home?

"I can imagine aught, but I couldnae say at this point. I might find contentment, but I dinna ken whether I can be happy with a philandering husband. It's nae that I would marry a mon I believe to be without honor. It's the humiliation of kenning everyone in the clan kens of his faithlessness. It's the humiliation of having to be near his women, of them kenning they are enough to make him stray from me. That I amnae enough to keep him in ma bed, and ma bed alone."

"It's nae too late to speak to Da. Ye ken he loves ye dearly and would never wish ye a miserable life. It's possible for him to decline the offer, and we all return home."

"Ye ken I canna ask that. The whole point of this marriage is to end the strife between our clans. Turning away now would just be an insult. I doubt Laird Mackay or Alan would stand for it. I'm as stuck here as I am in a bog." Mairghread heaved a heavy sigh and stood. With that, they exited the garden. They were just in time to watch Alan duck into the stables, pushing a giggling woman ahead of him.

Tristan couldn't get Mairghread out of his mind. Sitting at his desk in his solar with her father and three other brothers did little to lessen the distraction she posed. The five men had settled in to draft the betrothal contract. Tristan believed Alan should be present for this as it would be his marriage, but since he was showing Mairghread the gardens, it seemed fine to begin without him.

The men worked through the details for almost three hours before there was any agreement. At times, the conversation became tense, but Liam was adamant the dower lands he offered remain in trust for any daughters Mairghread and Alan might have. The Mackays weren't to use them other than for farming or grazing. He wouldn't permit them to place any crofts or keeps on the land if the Mackays were building them. The Sinclairs, without coming out and saying it, didn't want any Mackays making their home that close to the Sinclairs' land. The Sinclairs might form an alliance, but they didn't entirely trust the Mackays. Once again, the notion that Mairghread was the sacrificial lamb came floating into Tristan's mind.

Liam might trust the Mackays with his daughter's future, but he didn't trust them with the future of his land. Tristan would have been insulted on Mairghread's behalf if he hadn't already seen how much the man loved his daughter. He understood the laird was also doing this to safeguard Mairghread's future. If she were to die and Alan remarried, any daughters they had might be at risk of being sent off to a convent or given in a hurried marriage, so they wouldn't interfere with the new marriage. While he didn't foresee that happening in his lifetime, he was a laird and a warrior. He wasn't certain just how long that life might be. This land would be a safe dowry for those daughters. It would also be a place where Mairghread or her future daughters might go if they needed a different home. Tristan didn't foresee that eventuality either, but it made her father feel better. He wouldn't begrudge the man that. He imagined he might do the same if he had a daughter one day.

A daughter? Sons? I've been careful thus far to make sure I havenae had any. But one day. Will I find a woman as fair as Mairghread for maself? I will have to watch her marry ma arse of a stepbrother and grow round with his bairns. I will have to watch as he breaks her heart repeatedly with his cheating and drinking. God only kens how she'll be able to get along with Beatris. Mayhap she'll have the patience that I dinna. I'm torturing maself already. Mayhap she isnae as great as she seems. Mayhap I willna covet ma brother's wife once I ken the real Mairghread. This might all be for show, and a different side will come out once she settles here. Mayhap I will be the lucky one nae to have married her.

Even as these last thoughts ran through Tristan's head, his mind and heart screamed they were false. He was trying to talk himself out of the infatuation he was developing. Tristan had bedded his fair share of women, and then some. He wasn't some green lad chasing after his first skirt. At eight-and-twenty, he had almost half a lifetime of experience with women. Even with this experience, he couldn't shake how strongly his brother's intended drew him. Instinct told him Mairghread was as good and pure of heart and character as he had seen so far. If anything, he was certain he would find her even better as he got to know her.

Mayhap I ought to build a manor house for them somewhere beyond the crofts. Then they'd move there, and I wouldnae have to watch them together. I wouldnae need to see her every day if I provide them with servants. They'd live, sleep, and eat there. Alan would come up to the lists every day, and I would have to suffer through his bragging, but I wouldnae have to see her. Nae only would that solve seeing Mairghread, but I ken Beatris would follow them to the house. That alone would make this worthwhile.

Once again, Tristan understood these thoughts to be false. He couldn't relegate Mairghread to some manor house where it would force her to live in such a small space with her mother-by-marriage, her husband, and all the women he was bedding. At least the large keep might make it a little less obvious how many affairs his stepbrother would have over the years. That idea brought bile to the back of his throat, and he wanted to gag. Mairghread didn't deserve the husband they were about to stick her with.

"Laird Mackay? Didna ye hear what I said? I've said it thrice already," Liam said with impatience.

"Nay. Ma apologies, but ma mind wandered there for a

moment. I'm sorry, but could ye repeat yerself? Again." Tristan cringed a bit at that.

"I said, I would like to wait a fortnight before we sign this, and a moon before the wedding takes place. I would be sure this arrangement satisfies ma daughter before we make it permanent, and I leave her here in *yer* keeping."

Tristan recognized the stress on the word "your" meant the man had little faith in his stepbrother, and he would hold Tristan responsible for anything bad that might happen to Mairghread. He also understood once Alan wedded and bedded her, there would be little authority for him to do anything, since she would become Alan's property. Unless he beat her, there was no guarantee of a fulfilling marriage. He didn't want to be his brother's keeper, and he didn't think he would be successful banning Alan from sleeping with other women. Alan's deviousness would find a way around it. Tristan had considered having Alan marry before him in the hopes a wife and responsibilities to his own family would make Alan settle down. But it was obvious Tristan wasted his wishful thinking.

"Laird Sinclair, I will do ma vera best to ensure Mairghread is care of well here at Castle Varrich." That was the best offer Tristan could make. He noticed his pledge stating she would be taken care of at the keep, while not mentioning his stepbrother, didn't go undetected by Liam.

"Call me Liam. We are to be kin and allies soon." No mention of being friends. Tristan sighed.

"And ye can call me Tristan." *What the bluidy hell have I gotten maself into?*

The men exited the solar in time to watch Magnus and Mairghread enter the Great Hall. Tristan scanned the hall to determine if Alan was already inside or following behind them. He was nowhere in sight. It had been several hours since he entered his solar for the negotiations and Alan had taken Mairghread to the garden. He'd expected Alan to join them in the solar once they returned from the garden, but he never showed up.

Mairghread and Magnus walked up to their family and Laird Mackay. Tristan saw she'd gotten a few new freckles that day. The realization that he noticed was a bit unsettling to him, but he was sure of it. She smelled of lavender and heather and now fresh air. Her cheeks were pink, and her open-mouthed smiled showed two rows of perfectly shaped white teeth.

"Da, Firelight and Tavish found two mares they're rather fond of! Laird Mackay, ye might have two new foals on the way before ma kin leaves!" Mairghread laughed, and Tristan was certain it was the sound of a faerie's bell. He also didn't miss the term of affection for her father. Tristan paused, though. Something Mairghread said struck him as odd.

"Tavish?" Tristan looked at the brother who had been with him for the past three hours.

Mairghread laughed once again. "Aye. Tavish, the stallion." She looked at her brother and laughed even harder. "I mean Tavish, the horse, is rather taken with yer dappled mare, and ma horse rather fancies yer fawn-colored mare."

Tristan looked at the family, still in some confusion. "Ye have a horse and a brother named Tavish? I dinna ken how that is."

It was Magnus's turn to laugh now as Tavish, the brother, glared at him. It was a long running family joke and cause of annoyance for Tavish, the brother. "Tavish is ma horse. Da gave me the horse when I was seven. At the time, Tavish, over here, was ma favorite brother. A week later ma favorite changed, and I tried to change the horse's name to Callum, but it would only respond to Tavish. So, it stuck."

Tristan tried hard not to laugh, as he didn't want to do it at the other man's expense. It took a great deal of effort, and he almost choked. Tears twinkled in Mairghread's eyes as she looked over at Tristan.

"Go ahead and laugh. Ye ken ye're bursting to do it. The only one who never laughs is Tavish. Ma brother, nae the horse, that is." With that, she laughed again. Tristan could no longer contain it after hearing her infectious giggle. He chuckled, too. "Laird Mackay, ye have a wonderful stable. Ye have some of the best horses I've ever seen. Do ye breed many here? Or have ye found them elsewhere?"

"Lady Mairghread, are ye fond of horses?" It took Tristan aback that a lady would mention such a topic as horse breeding.

"Ma sister has been riding since she was auld enough to hold her head up. Da would take her out, wrapped in his plaid against his chest. She would look out and coo at everything and everyone. Once she sat up, she moved to riding in front of Da but still with his plaid wrapped around her to keep her close. She's been in the saddle since she was a bairn." This was the most Alexander had said since they arrived. Tristan hadn't been sure he talked at all.

"Alex, the laird was talking to me. I can answer for maself." Mairghread raised an eyebrow at her brother, but the corner of her mouth twitched.

"Laird Mackay—"

"Please, ye should all call me Tristan as we are soon-to-be kin."

"A-all right. Tristan, I do love horses. I love to ride, but I also like to take care of ma horse. And that includes where I send him to stud. I ken it is nae a normal topic for a woman to ken aboot, but with four aulder brothers, I couldnae nae learn aboot it." Mairghread caught herself stammering when Tristan told her to call him by his Christian name. She was unprepared for that or the sensations it caused. The name slid off her tongue as though she'd used it for years. It felt right. More so than the name Alan. That was a name she was rapidly disliking with a passion. *I'd rather ma passion go to Tristan. Jesu, Mary, and Joseph! Where did that come from? Bluidy bleeding hell! Argh! Now that's three times I've cursed and will have to confess. I must find out if they have a priest here sharpish. Willna that be nice? 'Hello, Father. I've nae yet been here a day and havenae even joined the clan yet, but I need to make a lengthy confession. Have ye time?' Wonderful."*

Tristan's voice brought her back to the present. She forced herself to focus on what he said rather than what she dreamed he might say to her—in private. "So, Alan showed ye the stables after the garden? Did ye three go anywhere else? I admit we left ye with quite a lot of time to fill on yer own."

Mairghread and Magnus shared a glance between them. It wasn't one that reassured Tristan. Mairghread spoke up. "Nay. Alan wasna the one to show us the stables. He walked there from the gardens, but we werenae the ones who were with him. I suspect he had some—er—something else to see to. Magnus and I wandered around the bailey, meeting yer clansmen and women until the stables were available for us to visit."

Tristan's heart sank with this. Mairghread didn't need to be any clearer to let everyone know Alan had a rendezvous with some woman in the stables when he was supposed to be getting to know Mairghread. Magnus now glared at Tristan, as he was the only Mackay available at present to receive his disdain.

Liam and his other three sons stared at Mairghread in disbelief. Callum finally spoke up. "Just how long did ye spend with yer intended? Ye away the three hours we were meeting."

"Magnus, what say ye? Alan was there aboot twenty minutes." Mairghread shrugged and plowed on ahead, hoping to change the subject. "Tristan, yer people were vera kind to me. Many stopped to talk with us, and I played catch with a few of the lads. I dinna imagine they've ever seen a lass throw as far as I can. It thrilled the lasses to watch me beat the lads. I admit I encouraged the lasses to give it a go and gave them some pointers on how to surely trounce the lads. I may have only befriended the younger females of yer clan so far, but Magnus had several of the aulder females wanting to make friends with him." Mairghread smirked at her brother as he reached out to pinch her side. She swatted at his hand.

Callum wasn't as eager to move on from Alan abandoning them on their walk. His clan knew him for his tenacity, and he wasn't ready to give up on this topic. "Mairghread, are ye telling us that out of three hours, ye spent only twenty minutes with Alan? Ye watched him go into the stables. I take it ye hinted it was with a woman other than yerself."

"Callum, of course, it was with someone else. I canna be in two places at once. I told ye, Magnus and I toured the bailey. Tristan, I should like to ride in the morning. Is it safe to ride in the meadow outside the gate? What aboot near the loch? Are there any bogs I should worry aboot?" Mairghread did her best to steer the conversation back around. She gave Callum a pointed look. One he returned but let the subject drop.

Tristan was unsure what to say at this point. He was so embarrassed by his stepbrother's behavior. He wanted it to be inconceivable that Alan would be so blatant in his dalliances, but he knew in his heart it didn't surprise him. Tristan looked down at Mairghread, seeing the hurt she was trying to hide. He recognized how she begged he would keep the conversation away from something so humiliating.

"Aye. Ye can ride out to the meadow and yon. I'm sure ye would like the loch. Yer horse can have a drink, and ye can sit on the rocks for a spell. Do ye ken how to skip rocks?"

"Are ye seriously asking me that?" Mairghread smirked. "Once again, I have four aulder brothers. How couldnae I ken how to skip rocks?"

"Mayhap yer brothers and da would like to join ye for yer ride, and I'll show ye all aboot."

Alexander had to put his two cents in. "Do ye think Alan might make himself available for such a tour? As laird, I'm sure ye have more pressing matters. I'd think Alan would like another opportunity to get to ken his bride and her kin."

"Right ye are. I will ask him at the evening meal. Lady Mairghread, I believe Lady Beatris is trying to get yer attention. I'd venture to say she'd like for ye to join her at the hearth. Do ye sew? I'd guess that's what she is doing now."

Mairghread looked to her father and noticed his scowl seemed to have become permanently etched on his face since arriving at the Mackays'. She gave an almost imperceptible nod before looking at Tristan. "Aye. I sew. I shall gather ma current piece of embroidery and join her in a moment." Mairghread dipped a curtsy and moved to the stairs.

"I think a dram of whisky might be in order," Tristan muttered as he motioned toward his solar.

CHAPTER 3

The evening meal progressed nicely, and it seemed the lairds' families were getting along. While Alan still shoveled food and wine into his mouth as though he feared someone would steal his trencher, he did at least leave a decent portion for Mairghread. As befitting a soon-to-be betrothed couple, they shared one. At first, Mairghread thought Alan was being kind with the choicest pieces of venison and pheasant going into the trencher, but she realized these were landing on his side. He plunked down any piece he found on top when he got around to serving her. The juices would have splattered and ruined her kirtle if she hadn't grabbed the edge of the tablecloth to cover her lap. She never got a drop to drink, as they also shared a goblet. Alan hoarded it as though he would soon expire from thirst. Mairghread had seen plenty of men drink wine or ale with their meals, but Alan alternated back and forth, depending on which buxom serving wench was near to hand. If it was a homely-looking woman, he didn't wave her over as his goblet emptied, but if the woman was comely, he pulled her into his lap to pour another serving. He was well into his cups by the third course.

Mairghread plastered her most serene smile on her face as she suffered through the meal. As though Alan's manners and behavior weren't bad enough, Beatris sat on Mairghread's other side. She kept rambling on about Alan's many accomplishments. From what Mairghread could tell, they weren't accomplishments, rather Alan doing the very least people expected of him, and his boastful mother's exaggerations. Beatris spoke of how he learned to read and write well enough that he no longer needed lessons after the age of ten, even though Tristan needed to continue with a tutor until he was seven-and-ten. She didn't see the point of why Tristan learned to read and write Gaelic, English, and Latin. She, herself, had survived five-and-forty years without being able to read and write any of those languages.

According to Beatris, Alan had learned to sit a horse by the age of five and rode better than all the other guardsmen, or so she claimed. She was sure to tell Mairghread that Alan was the strongest of all the clansmen, and he shot an arrow farther and straighter than any other man in the Highlands. Mairghread wanted to laugh outright at the comment about his strength. She had met Tristan and seen the blacksmith and his apprentices. Alan was far from being the strongest man in the clan. Had the woman not seen Mairghread's own brothers? As for his prowess with a bow and arrow, perhaps when he was sober. At the moment, he was so drunk he barely raised the goblet or eating knife to his mouth without missing.

As the meal finished, the clansmen moved the trestle tables aside, and musicians played. The meal was a small feast to celebrate Clan Sinclair's arrival and the upcoming betrothal. Alan burped and patted his belly but made no move to invite Mairghread to dance. Tristan knew he couldn't be the first one to invite her. That role should have gone to Alan. As couples moved onto the floor, he observed the wistful expression upon her face. Mairghread wanted to dance, and she swayed to the music. After a few minutes, Tavish rose and took her by the hand to lead her onto the floor. They joined the others for a lively country reel. Soon Tristan recognized Mairghread's laughter in the crowd as her hair flew behind her, and she kicked up her heels. She danced two more songs with her brother before Callum, Alexander, and Magnus each claimed a dance.

"Alan, go dance with yer intended. Ye might at least pretend to pay her a bit of attention," Tristan whispered.

"Why? Ye've already drafted the agreement with her father. The deal is as good as done. I have nay need for her except to bear me sons. Since she canna do that right this moment, I shall continue as I am."

The heat rising along Tristan's neck and into his face scorched him. He wanted nothing more in this moment than to throttle his stepbrother and smash his fist into his face. "Ye will go out and dance with Lady Mairghread. Ye will make her feel welcome. Ye will behave yerself and nae shame this clan. Or ye willna ever drink another drop in this keep. *Now go!*" Tristan veritably barked his order to Alan. His stepbrother looked up at him. He had his perpetual sneer on his face. It was the countenance Tristan recognized meant he would do what he wanted despite any consequences. His demeanor told Tristan Alan was beyond reason.

Please let him behave with even a modicum of decency.

Alan made his way to the dance floor but stopped to flirt with three different women on the way. He promised to meet one of them in the storeroom behind the kitchens after the music ended. He stole a sloppy kiss from another. In his stupor, he didn't realize and didn't care that each Sinclair—the laird's family and guardsmen alike—observed his behavior before he came to Mairghread's side. She was dancing with Auld Michael, one of the clan's elders.

"Move on auld mon. I've come for ma woman."

Auld Michael gave Mairghread an apologetic look and seemed to linger.

"It's all right, Michael. I've been expecting to dance with Alan."

Auld Michael moved away, but not before hearing Alan's hoarse whisper, "What the hell was that supposed to mean?"

"Naught. I hoped at some point we might dance together."

Alan grasped her around the waist and yanked her into him. Something hard bumped against her front, and she was positive it was too low to be his abdomen and too high to be his thigh. She almost shuddered with disgust. He hadn't been near her long enough for her to cause it. Someone else had clearly aroused him. Which of the three women she saw made him stand at attention she didn't know, nor did she care. He held her roughly as they moved around the dance floor.

"Ye're a sweet piece of fluff, are nae ye, ma sweet? Ye'll do well warming ma bed each night. Dinna think ye shall sleep alone often. Ye'll be in ma bed every night that I want ye. On those nights I want someone else, ye may sleep in another chamber... Or ye could watch, if ye fancy." Alan leaned forward and licked Mairghread's ear. She struggled not to throw up. "We're all but married at this point. Give me a taste of what's to come. Come with me to ma chamber and show me what I'll have every night after we stand before the kirk."

Alan grabbed her backside and thrust his hips forward. His other hand snuck between them to squeeze Mairghread's breast. His hand grazed her right breast just before she stepped back and thrust her right knee into his groin. When he gasped and bent forward with his hand over his crotch, she threw her left elbow into his nose. Blood shot out all over and splattered her kirtle.

"Ye bluidy bitch. Ye broke ma nose! Ye'll pay for yer insolence."

Mairghread flicked her right wrist, and a dirk appeared in

her hand. She lowered her hand, so the point of the dirk was at his groin. "Take a step closer, and I'll saw off yer twig and berries."

"Ye dinna have the nerve. Ye wouldnae dare. Ye're naught but a cock tease. Ye—"

Mairghread cut him short when she flicked her left wrist, and another dirk appeared. This one she aimed at his throat. "I wouldnae keep insulting me if ye'd like to keep yer bollocks or yer throat in one piece."

At first, Tristan could only tell there was some commotion on the floor. Once Alan's voice floated to him, he was certain it involved Mairghread, and Alan had done something wrong. As he rose, he listened to five other chairs being pushed back. Each shot back so hard it fell over. Then there was the sound of five swords being drawn. As Tristan rushed around the table, he watched Alexander and Magnus leap across the table, followed by Callum and Tavish. Liam ran around. All five surged forward and leaped from the dais. At the sight of their laird and his sons with drawn swords, the Sinclair guardsmen drew dirks and *sgian dubhs* from various places on their bodies. In response, the Mackay guardsmen drew theirs. Most clans didn't allow swords in the Great Hall apart from the laird's family, personal guard, and guests. This was why.

Tristan ran forward but came to a screeching halt when he took in the scene before him: Mairghread with two dirks pointing at his stepbrother, and Alan with a broken nose and a hand adjusting his groin.

"What is the meaning of this?" Liam roared. "What the hell did ye do to ma daughter that she had to defend herself from ye?"

"I didna do a damn thing wrong. Yer whore of a daughter teased me and then denied me ma due as her betrothed."

"Da—"

"Silence, Mairghread!" The Sinclair stepped up to Alan and

placed his face only inches from Alan's. At over a head taller, Liam had to lean down. "Ye dare call ma daughter a bitch, a cock tease, and a whore? I will kill ye right on the spot."

Tristan had to step in before this turned into a bloodbath. He looked around as the Sinclair guardsmen inched forward, ready to defend any of the laird's family who might be in need. Tristan didn't miss the white-hot fury on each of their faces. He noticed his own guardsmen were on the defensive, but it was to protect the clansmen and women. They had inched away. They had no intention of coming to Alan's rescue.

Doesnae that nae only speak volumes but scream it too? "Mairghread, tell us what happened, please." Tristan stepped in front of Mairghread to look at her. Her calm was remarkable, considering she was a foot shorter and at least ten stones lighter than Alan. She looked up at him with her blue-gray eyes. They were a darker gray than before. They reminded him of a storm cloud about to unleash a blizzard.

"He yanked me against him, then ground his staff into me. Someone else had clearly already entertained him when he interrupted ma dance with Auld Michael. Then he grabbed ma backside and one of ma breasts. Alan said I should give him a taste of what he'd be getting after the kirking. He said, since we're practically betrothed, it was his right. He also told me how I'd warm his bed every night another woman wasna already in it." Mairghread leaned around his shoulder and glared at Alan. She looked ready to spit fire. Tristan thought he had never seen a more remarkable woman.

"He said all of that, lass? Aught more?"

"Nay. Isnae that enough? I canna remember aught else."

"Ye're bluidy right that was more than enough! The Sinclairs ride out at dawn. There will be nay betrothal. Laird Mackay, count yerself lucky I respect ye, even if yer brother is a piece of shite. If I didna, I'd raze yer fields from here to the Orkney," Liam bellowed.

Out of nowhere came the shrill yell of Beatris, and Tristan's heart sank even further, if it was possible.

For Jesu's sake, could this get any worse?

"What did that hateful wench do to ye, son? Let me see ye. That trollop is a tease. I watched her at the table and the way she tried to entice ye with more food and drink. She's to blame for this."

Anyone who saw the diners at the dais knew this to be ridiculousness. Everyone observed how Alan behaved. Everyone knew how Alan behaved. There didn't seem to be a single face in the crowd moved by Beatris's claims.

"Woman, haud yer wheesht," Tristan snapped. "Dinna fash at Lady Mairghread for Alan's disgusting behavior."

"Tristan! How could ye speak out against yer own brother? How could ye betray me, yer own mother?"

"Ma brother, nay, ma *stepbrother* and ma *stepmother* will retire now." Tristan turned to face Alan, who moved to swing at Tristan, but Tristan wrapped his hand around Alan's throat. Being almost half a head taller and stronger, Tristan almost lifted Alan off his feet.

"Ye would insult our guests and then attempt to strike yer laird? Ye are through here tonight. Guards, escort Alan and Beatris to their chambers. Lock the doors from the outside and post men there throughout the night."

When he released him, Alan attempted to shove past Tristan and lunged at Mairghread. "Bitch!"

Tristan pushed Mairghread behind him and stepped between them. His hand shot out and slammed into Alan's jaw. Tristan had never heard a sound more satisfying than the crunch of his stepbrother's jaw breaking. Alan collapsed, and Beatris screamed. Tristan looked at his guardsmen, who had come forward. They collected both Alan and Beatris and removed them from the Great Hall.

Liam rushed forward and wrapped his daughter in his arms.

Mairghread melted into his embrace and clung to him. She shook as all the energy drained from her, and she was certain she would dissolve into nothing but a puddle if her father didn't continue to hold her up. When he stepped back, she dipped her head, so no one witnessed the tears now streaming down her face. She wouldn't have any of these people believe her weak. When she was a bit more composed, she looked up at her father. He gave her a tiny nod of the head. Tristan caught sight of it.

Ah, now I ken where she gets that mannerism from. The apples didna fall far from that tree.

"Lady Mairghread, ma apologies canna go far enough after what just happened, but I offer them to ye, anyway. I am so vera sorry. I ken ye bathed already, but if ye would like, I'll have another bath sent up to ye and mayhap a hot toddy to help ye sleep."

"Thank ye, Tristan. I willna have anyone hauling up a tub and hot water for me at this late hour. I would take that tot of whisky though." She was too drained to realize she addressed him by his Christian name in front of his clan. Magnus pushed past and elbowed Tristan in the ribs. Tristan was about to shove the person back until he realized it was Magnus. Magnus looked stricken to see his sister in such a state. While the other Sinclair men still looked ready to do bloody murder, Magnus looked as if he would be ill. He scooped Mairghread into his arms and moved toward the stairs without a word. "Magnus, I'm tired but nae broken. I can walk on ma own. Put me down. Now!"

Magnus looked at her and shook his head.

The Great Hall cleared of all those who would return to their crofts. Those who remained bedded down for the night, and snores rumbled from all corners of the room. Tristan was very ready for that drink he had promised himself hours ago. As he turned toward his solar, he spotted the last person he wanted to deal with now. Sorcha headed straight to him. And it was clear she was on a mission. He'd been bedding Sorcha for the better part of two years. While she was satisfying between the sheets, she was also a social climber. She kept hinting she should have the official label of the chief's leman. Tristan recognized what she wanted was to become the lady of the keep. Neither would happen.

While Sorcha was beautiful and satisfied his lust, Tristan had no intention of making their arrangement anything more serious or in any way permanent. He was aware she was cold to the other servants in the keep, and she would never fulfill the duties of the lady of the keep. Never mind the fact that marriage to her would bring no dowry or alliance to his clan. Tristan had never formally kept a leman, even though there were two other women he once had a long-standing agreement with. He was unwilling to commit to any woman enough to give her that much influence over him, or to believe she had authority over the members of the clan.

Tristan watched her approach. The normal surge of lust he experienced when she was near was missing now. She did nothing to stir him or his cock. Just the opposite. Tristan dreaded having her near him. Her scent of roses was cloying and sickening to him after the light fragrance of Mairghread's lavender and heather. Sorcha was aware she was an extremely attractive woman. She had long, wavy blond hair with blue eyes and an ample bosom. The latter she had on display for him now. The ties to the front of her kirtle were half undone, and she was practically falling out of her gown. She stopped in front of him and reached out to run her hands over his chest. It was her normal greeting, but this time Tristan grasped her wrists before she touched him.

"Sorcha, tis nae a good time."

"But ma laird, ye ken I can always make it a good time." Sorcha purred as she stepped closer.

Tristan took an instinctive step back. With sudden clarity, he was certain of what he needed to do. As he looked at Sorcha, there was nothing but an overwhelming desire to find Mairghread. He wanted to hold the lass with the chestnut hair, with streaks of fire running through it, just as those flames ran through her spirit. He had once found Sorcha's blond hair enticing. He'd enjoyed seeing it draped across his shoulders as she rode him, or when he wrapped it in his hand as he took her from behind. Now it seemed mousy compared to Mairghread's. He'd once enjoyed flicking his tongue against Sorcha's lips to prod them open as his tongue dueled with hers. Now he only remembered the fresh mint scent that always seemed to come from Mairghread's perfectly shaped, pinky-red lips.

"Sorcha, this canna happen now. This willna happen again. Our arrangement has seen its course and is now at an end."

"What?" Sorcha screeched. Tristan looked around the hall to make sure no one noticed. He had no intention of pulling her into a dark alcove for privacy because she would launch herself at him. While his mind wanted nothing to do with her, he wasn't so convinced his body would stay in agreement.

"Lass, I've enjoyed our time together. Ye ken that to be the truth. But this situation with Alan and the Sinclairs has made me realize I'll be needing a wife soon. I willna bring a woman to this keep to take to wife if I have another woman here who I'm bedding. I willna do that to any potential wife. That means our time together is done."

With that, Tristan turned toward his solar. He left a fuming Sorcha staring at him. If he'd stayed any longer or looked back, he would have seen the pure hate and malice that shone in her eyes. It would have forewarned him that a woman scorned was a dangerous enemy to make.

CHAPTER 4

Mairghread tossed all night long. The chamber was spacious and warm without being stifling. The bed was among the most comfortable she had ever touched, but her mind wouldn't settle despite how weary her mind and body were. She had been convinced the journey to Mackay land would never end, but now she wished she never arrived. Her mind kept replaying the events of the previous day. What she found most disturbing was her memory kept rushing back to her interactions with Tristan more often than her interactions with Alan. While she held nothing but contempt for Alan, she couldn't help the warmth that spread across her whenever she pictured Tristan. She pictured him as she first saw him as she entered the Great Hall.

Tristan appeared such a hulking figure at first that Mairghread wondered, before her eyes unadjusted to the dimness, if she were seeing a shadow cast along the wall. She realized it wasn't a shadow but a towering, braw man who took her breath away. Then she remembered him as she and Magnus returned to the keep. Her heart ached for him as he tried so extremely hard to make up for his stepbrother's disinterest in her. Her mind conjured him as he pushed her behind him for protection and grasped Alan around the throat after he insulted her for the last time. She couldn't stop the gasp that came out each time she pictured him slamming his fist into Alan's jaw. He'd been so kind to offer another bath to help her calm and looked so earnest when he gazed into her eyes. She had almost swooned then. Not from her confrontation with Alan. Not from the stares of all the people surrounding them. But from the warmth and concern she saw in his eyes.

It was almost sunrise when Mairghread opened her eyes once again. She had eventually drifted off, but she didn't feel well rested. Quickly, she rose and dressed. Mairghread gathered the few belongings she brought with her and placed them back in her trunk. She would break her fast before the others awoke because it was a certainty her father would want to be off, insisting upon eating on the road. She knew she wouldn't last that long. She stumbled headfirst over a log blocking her door when she opened it. However, logs didn't groan, nor did they move on their own. Through the dim torch light of the passageway, she saw two piercing green eyes staring up at her.

"Tristan? What are ye doing outside of ma door? Ye canna be here. It isnae proper."

"I couldnae sleep kenning ye might feel unsafe in ma keep. I came to guard yer door, so ye would ken ye're safe."

"Thank ye."

"I listened to ye moving aboot last night. I ken ye didna sleep well. I canna help but feel responsible for that." Mairghread blushed, knowing he'd been close enough to recognize what she did in bed. She looked past him to the stairs. Part of her wanted to make a mad dash for them to escape this conversation, and another part of her never wanted to leave that spot if it meant they continued standing together. "Lass, I ken ye and yer kin are aboot to leave, but I hoped ye might walk with me for a spell. I would like to speak with ye aboot something."

"Vera well. Lead on." Mairghread didn't think twice about following. Tristan extended his arm to point toward the stairs, but rather than go down to the Great Hall and out to the bailey, he led them up the stairs. Mairghread assumed he would take them to the battlements. He wouldn't take her to his chamber, would he? As they reached the third floor, Mairghread looked down the hallway. What she saw, or rather what she didn't see, stunned her. She turned accusing eyes on Tristan, her anger radiating from her.

"They're gone, lass. I didna send their guard away. I sent them away."

"What do ye mean?"

"I couldnae sleep either. Nae even after more than a dram of whiskey. It bothered me that they remained in ma keep. I ken it sends a message to all that I ultimately condone Alan's behavior, even if he and Beatris were under lock and key. I had a score of guardsmen escort them to a vacant croft at the edge of the village. They will have left aboot an hour ago for Beatris's clan. They can have them back. Neither Alan nor Beatris have any claim to remaining here. I allowed them to stay out of a sense a duty. I realize now it was a misplaced."

"Ye sent them off in the middle of the night? That seems rather dangerous to them and yer guardsmen."

"Ma guardsmen are used to traveling in the dark since they've each patrolled ma lands for years. I kenned ye would leave with the sun, and ye must travel some of the same route as they will. I didna want to risk ye and yer kin catching up to them on the trail."

"Tristan, that was vera kind of ye. I dinna ken what to say."

They had reached the top of the next flight of narrow stairs that led out to the battlements. While the days were warm since it was summer, the moon provided no such warmth. The sun still hadn't appeared yet. Tristan regretted not suggesting Mairghread gather her arisaid. He unfastened the clan brooch at his shoulder and released the extra length of plaid.

"I ken it isnae proper, but I dinna want ye to catch a chill while we are up here." Tristan stood beside her and held out the plaid. Mairghread paused and looked into his eyes. He realized she must have been confident in what she observed, because she sidestepped closer to him. He wrapped the plaid around her shoulders and kept his arm around them, too. Unconsciously, she leaned into his heat. He was warmer than a blazing fire. Her side that touched his quickly warmed, and the contact sent a shiver down her spine. Tristan mistook it as a sign she was still cold, so he gently pulled her closer to him. She wasn't about to protest.

"Mairghread, there's something I would like to talk to ye aboot. I still feel exceedingly bad aboot how ma bro—stepbrother treated ye. Ye didna deserve any of it. I dinna want ye to remember this as how all Mackay men treat women."

Mairghread turned to stand in front of Tristan. They stood cocooned within Tristan's *breacan feile*, or great plaid, and her chest absorbed his heat. It seemed to seep inside her and spread down to her belly, then her lady parts below. His saffron leine was open at the neck, and she noticed his smooth chest beneath it. Her fingers itched to touch the revealed skin. She wondered if it would be as smooth as it looked. As she gazed up, she noticed a lock of his ebony hair had fallen over his eyebrow. It took every bit of her self-control not to reach up and brush it back off his forehead. "Tristan, I never considered Alan's actions were that of all Mackay men. I dinna believe ma da or ma brothers think that either."

"Even after all what happened yesterday, I canna say I regret that ye came. I regret I promised ye to ma stepbrother. Promised ye to him rather than to me."

The arm that was around Mairghread's shoulder had, at some point, slid down to wrap around her waist. Tristan felt her soft intake of air, then her mint scented breath fanned across his face. He struggled to withstand the temptation she created by being so close, but he refused to act in any way that might remind her of Alan.

"I have to admit I dinna want ye to leave here, nae today and nae any day after. I would ask ye to consider something. I've been drawn to ye since the moment I laid eyes on ye. I canna seem to stop thinking aboot ye, and I have found maself impressed with ye many times over, Mairghread. Ye have a keen mind and a sharp sense of humor. I've seen ye with ma clan, and many of them have already told me they like ye. That isnae a simple thing to accomplish in so short a time. Ye ken Highlanders arenae often welcoming to outsiders, but a good number have already told me they're glad ye've come. They ken ye're kind and warm-hearted. I ken it, too. I would ask ye to consider staying on for a bit. I would like to discover if we suit. If ye're of the opinion that we do, and we agree, then I would ask ye to marry me. I dinna want to miss this opportunity with ye. I reckon ye may be just the right woman for me. I—"

Mairghread reached up and placed one soft finger on Tristan's lips. She smiled up at him, and his cock twitched. It came alive the moment he wrapped his arm around her and saw his plaid draped over her. Now it was fully awake, and it ached to press against her. Once again, he held himself in check. He would do nothing to jeopardize this moment.

"I'm drawn to ye as well, Tristan. The idea of marrying Alan but seeing ye every day was unpleasant but kenning that one day ye would marry another was torture. I wasna sure how I could do it. I kept trying to tell maself that what a braw mon ye are simply impressed me, and that it's naught but infatuation. But I dinna suppose it is just infatuation. Ye dinna have to try so hard to convince me."

"Ye think I'm a braw mon?"

"Is that all ye heard of what I said?" Mairghread raised one eyebrow and pursed her lips, but Tristan caught the mirth in her eyes.

"Nay, Mair. I heard all ye had to say. I dinna consider it infatuation on ma part either."

Mairghread liked the term of endearment. She'd never had one before. Her brothers had several nicknames for her growing up, some of which still stuck, but no one had used her actual name to come up with one.

"Tristan, ye will have to convince ma da to let me stay. I can try, but it must be ye who shows him I'll be well treated here. I doubt his anger will have calmed much, even now. Ma brothers are another case, too. Even if Da agrees for the sake of the alliance, I dinna ken if ma brothers will ever let Da leave me here."

"I understand. If I had a daughter or a sister who meant as much to me as ye do to them, I would have committed bluidy murder last night. They would leave neither Alan nor I standing. Mair, I would ask one last thing of ye before we go belowstairs." Tristan took a noticeably deep breath and swallowed. "Would ye let me kiss ye? I think that would be a good place to start if we are to figure out if we suit."

Mairghread caught herself holding her breath. She lifted her chin as she looked up at Tristan. He put his thumb and forefinger on her chin as he lowered his head. Mairghread had a sinking sensation this wasn't a wise choice. Not because she didn't trust him, but because she didn't trust herself. "Wait."

"What? What do ye mean?"

"I dinna think we should kiss. Nae yet at least." Mairghread hurried to get her explanation out as she watched the surprise turn to hurt in his eyes. "Tristan, I want to kiss ye. I want it rather badly, almost—nay, most definitely—too much. If we kiss, and we enjoy it, then it will lead to more kissing. That's nae an altogether bad thing, but I want to ken if we suit. I dinna doubt we would suit physically. I ken how attracted I am to ye, and I sense ye are at least a wee attracted to me. If we kiss, I'm afraid the physical side of our relationship will become too much of the focus. I willna always look like this. One day, I will have bairns. I will gain weight and nae all of it may come off afterwards. Ma hair will gray, and I will get wrinkles. If the only thing that binds us is our physical desire, then what will we do when that fades? I need to ken we have a real foundation for a marriage. Does that make sense to ye?"

"Aye, *mo chaileag*. It does."

Mairghread jerked back. "Tristan, please one thing before ye go on. Alan called me 'ma sweet,' and it made ma skin crawl. I dinna ever want someone to call me that or aught close to it again."

"Vera well, little one. I willna ever call ye that, even if one day I find out that's how ye taste. And I will wait to find out until ye say we are ready. Ye're wise beyond yer years. I agree if we are to get to ken one another to determine whether we are right for one another, then kissing and cuddling can come later." Tristan placed a chaste kiss on her forehead. "That shall have to last me for now. We had better go belowstairs. Yer da should be up by now, and I dinna want him tearing ma keep apart looking for ye."

"Tristan, there is one other thing before this can go any further. I must ken something aboot ye." He saw the seriousness in her eyes, and he straightened to his full height. This made him a foot taller than Mairghread. But she didn't seem intimidated in the least. In turn, this made him nervous about what she would ask. "If we marry, will ye be faithful to me?"

Mairghread might have knocked him over with a feather. It wasn't a question he expected, but after what she saw with Alan, it was a fair one. "Mairghread, in ma heart, marriage is sacred. I wouldnae stray from ye or any woman I marry. I would never dishonor ye by doing that."

Tristan took a breath before he continued. What he was

about to tell her might stop their relationship before it even began. He'd intended to tell her, but not quite this soon after asking her to stay on. Perhaps it was for the best that it come out now.

"I wasna going to say aught aboot this yet. But I ken I must now, and it'll be for the best. Until last night, I was involved with a woman here in the keep. She wasna exactly ma leman, but she has filled that role many times over the past two years. After ye retired, I headed to ma solar for a dram—or four—of whisky. She approached me and offered to keep me company. I looked down at her, and all I could see was that she wasna ye. She didna appeal to me in the least. I couldnae get away fast enough. I ended things with her, but she doesnae ken it's because of ye that I nay longer want her. I said I would have to marry soon, and after Alan's actions, I have nay desire to be aught like him. I couldnae and wouldnae have a woman in the keep who might consider me a future husband while keeping a leman." Tristan held his breath as his heart raced. For the second time that morning, he'd rambled and blurted out everything he could think to tell Mairghread.

"That is quite a lot to take in. I'm glad ye told me before I found out aboot whomever this woman is. I take it she works in the keep and is someone I'll have to deal with often if I become the chatelaine. If I become the lady of the clan, then she will work for me. That may nae go over well with her, or any of the other women ye've been with who live and work in the keep." Mairghread looked up at Tristan and asked pointedly, "Are there many of them I will have to encounter day to day? Are there many here who will ken ye better than I will come our wedding day?"

"Mairghread, there are only two other women besides this one who were aught close to a leman. I granted none of the privileges a leman often enjoys. None have ever shared the laird's bed with me. I will be honest that there are women in the village and beyond who I've gotten to ken beyond passing glances. I willna ever flaunt ma past in yer face, but I canna guarantee ye willna have to deal with these women."

"I ken ye have a past, and I'm only a recent addition to ye life. I hope we suit, and I can be a permanent addition. All I can ask is there be nay others from now on. Nae during this time while we figure out if we will wed, and if we do, then nae after that either."

"Ye have ma word of honor on that. I want nay other, and I will have nay other." Tristan pulled her into his chest and hugged her tightly. He might not kiss her, but he would enjoy having her in his embrace, even if only for a moment. Mairghread didn't hesitate to return his hug by wrapping her arms around him as best she could. She rested her head against his heart and listened to its steady rhythm. She sighed as she felt safe with him. The same sense of belonging she got when she embraced her father or brothers seeped into her marrow. But this was different, too. Desire heated her belly again, and an ache developed between her legs. Her breasts were heavy, and she longed to press her hips forward. She was aware he was aroused too, but unlike with Alan, she wanted to feel his stiff shaft pressed against her. They stood like that for several minutes before they both accepted that they had to pull away and return to the Great Hall.

"Da! Ye arenae listening to me! Please stop saddling yer horse and listen to me."

"Mairghread, ye're late coming down here. A stable lad has already seen to yer horse. Get on. We leave *now*."

"Nay!"

Liam turned around slowly and stared down at his youngest child. "What did ye say? I havenae time for yer nonsense aboot staying on. If ye didna get enough sleep and are too tired to ride alone, then ye can ride with one of yer brothers. If ye are hungry, then ye should have come down sooner. Ye can eat a bannock once we set off. Now mount yer horse so we can be off." He vaulted himself into the saddle.

"Da! I amnae going anywhere."

"What are ye blathering on aboot, lass?"

"Are ye ready to listen to me? I'd ask ye get down, so I might have a word without every ear in this keep hearing me."

Liam and his sons all dismounted and moved over to where Mairghread stood at the foot of the keep's steps. She had already tried to get her father's attention as she arrived in the Great Hall with Tristan at her side, but her father and brothers were striding to the door. Mairghread ran to catch up with them, calling out to her father four times and asking him to wait each time. She kept saying she wanted to stay, but he shook his head and kept marching forward. Once her father and brothers stepped toward her and Tristan, she moved back to stand at Tristan's side. This didn't go unnoticed by her family. Five sets of chestnut eyebrows shot upwards. Five scowls were directed at Tristan. Five sets of knuckles clenched at their sides.

"Da, I didna say aught yesterday, as there wasna a point at the time. I didna hold any hope aught might come of it, but I am seriously interested in Tristan. I told maself he would make a fine friend and mayhap an ally once I married his stepbrother. I didna want to marry Alan, but I would for the clan. I didna like kenning I would marry one mon while interested in another, but I would have done it for our people. Now I dinna have to. Tristan sent his stepbrother and stepmother away early this morn. He sent a score of warriors with them to escort them back to Lady Beatris's clan. Tristan has asked me to consider being his wife. He asked me to stay on for a while, so we might spend some time getting to ken one another and to figure out if we suit. I'd like to stay."

"And just how did ye come by this information so early in the morn? Ye came down the stairs with Laird Mackay at yer side, and now ye refer to him as Tristan. Just what happened after ye supposedly retired?"

Tristan stepped in front of Mairghread and threw his shoulders back. He took a wide stance and put his fists on his hips. He was aware he was an intimidating man, but he was matched up against five other equally intimidating men. "I dinna like what ye're implying aboot yer daughter. She has done naught to receive such censure from ye. It is as she says. Alan and Beatris left the keep last night and rode out for Clan MacDonnell over two hours ago. I wanted to be sure Mair was well and safe, so I slept *outside* her door last night once I'd given ma orders for Alan and Beatris. When Mair arose this morn, she found me outside her door. She agreed to speak with me for a while, and we discussed her staying on. I hope it to be permanent."

"Ye defend ma daughter, but just where did this chat happen? Ye were nae in the passageway when we each exited our chambers. And ye were nae at the dais to break yer fast. So where were ye?"

"Ye're implying yer daughter and I might have been somewhere we shouldnae have been, and I resent that because it isnae the case." Tristan turned to point above his head at the wall walk. "We were on the battlements. It's a place I like to go to think. I wanted us to have a moment to think."

"Da, I want to stay. I didna want to come here at all, but I did as ye told me. Now, I'm asking ye to listen to what I want. I ken ye're still angry aboot last night and aboot Alan. But I ken ye can tell Alan and Tristan are naught alike. And I call him Tristan because he gave me and all of ye leave to do so yesterday."

The wind seemed to leave Liam's sail as he looked at the hopeful expression on his daughter's face. He wasn't a man who didn't tell his daughter no. He had done it many times over the years, but this was one of the few times she asked for something for her and her alone. She always placed her kin and clan ahead of herself. Liam had been heartsick all day as he watched Alan, so it relieved him when an obvious reason came for him to pack up his children and leave. He'd been ready to find any excuse even remotely believable to extricate his daughter from the potential marriage. He would have even surrendered her dowry if it meant taking her home and keeping the peace. He realized now that this might just be the right solution. A marriage to a laird would forge a stronger alliance than one to a laird's stepbrother. More importantly, it seemed to be a marriage that would benefit his daughter, not her station.

"Aye." Liam sighed and rubbed his forehead. "We'll stay on. But ma terms have changed. I dinna want to wait just a fortnight to sign the betrothal contract. We shall wait a full moon. If I sign it, then we shall wait at least two more moons before ye wed. Are we willing to host us that long?"

"Aye, Liam. Three moons or longer if that's what it takes to prove maself a worthy husband for yer daughter."

CHAPTER 5

The next fortnight flew by in a whirlwind for both Mairghread and Tristan. They settled into a routine, and it seemed Mairghread was already the lady of the keep. With Beatris gone, not that she had ever fulfilled the duties well, Mairghread stepped in. She worked with the sisters Annag, the cook, and Morag, the housekeeper, to set the menu and oversee the keep's maintenance.

The second day of helping the servants made Mairghread realize she needed to investigate the castle accounts. Beatris had poorly managed things in the storerooms with some provisions overstocked, while others were too depleted. Tristan handed the ledgers over to her without hesitation, and she spent an afternoon in his solar pouring over them. Since Beatris never learned to read or write, and the kitchen staff couldn't either, the ledgers were a mess. Beatris had made what looked like chicken scratches to tally items, but there were so many inaccuracies that Mairghread lost count. In fact, she gave up count. She reverted to the beginning of the year and attempted to make corrections. It took her almost four hours of painstaking work to bring the records to her satisfaction. Afterward, she made a thorough inventory of all the storerooms in the keep. That took her the rest of the afternoon and into midmorning the next day.

Throughout the chores, Mairghread was kind to the kitchen and housekeeping servants. She asked questions to learn their methods and routines. She did her best not to change anything that wasn't absolutely necessary. She wanted to fit in, not overrun them. Once she was confident the kitchen was in order, she began an inventory of other household goods such as candles and linens. She realized immediately that they were running low on candles.

Even though it was still summer, she understood the days would soon grow shorter. They would need an ample stock of candles to see the clan through winter. Much to the surprise and even shock of many of the servants, Mairghread brought out all the supplies and set them up on a trestle table in the Great Hall. Then she rolled up her sleeves and got to work. No noblewoman had helped make candles since the current laird's father's mother had been alive. When they finished the candles and stored them away, Mairghread turned her attention to the castle's laundresses.

Mairghread met them early one morning after breaking her fast. She approached and picked up a wet sheet and pinned it to the line. After she did three more, she turned to find all the women gawking at her. "Can ye nae use an extra set of hands?"

It took a moment before anyone formulated an answer, but Aignes, the head washerwoman, stepped forward. "Ma lady, ye're a noblewoman and a guest here. We canna have ye working in the laundry. It just isnae done."

"Aignes, isnae it? I've been helping hang laundry since I was auld enough to climb on an overturned bucket and reach the lines. I'm happy to help ye, if ye'll let me."

The women all looked at each other, then at Mairghread's smiling face. They nodded and got back to work. She blended into the group so well the women forgot who she was. Mairghread soon picked up all the juiciest pieces of gossip. By the nooning, she learned which wife would have a redheaded bairn when she and her husband both had brown hair. The young women pointed to which guardsman had put on a disappointing display for a woman he'd been chasing for months. She discovered which families had sick children and which families were struggling. It was these last pieces of information that she tucked away to discuss with Tristan later.

And so, each morning during that first fortnight progressed similarly, just as the afternoons did. Mairghread would break her fast with her family and Tristan. The men went to the lists to train, and Mairghread remained to tend to her duties and chores. The men sometimes returned for the noon meal, but at other times, they ate on the training field. However, no matter where Tristan took his midday meal, he always returned to spend the afternoon with Mairghread.

It took the clan two days to realize the reason the Sinclairs stayed on. The laird was courting Lady Mairghread. It was the clan's consensus that she was a wise choice. She was openhearted to everyone she met, but she was also among the hardest working people who labored in and around the keep. There wasn't a job she wouldn't do if it needed doing. She never asked more of anyone than she would do herself. The clan realized Mairghread didn't agree there was any job beneath her. They approved wholeheartedly, since it was a reprieve from Beatris.

In the afternoons, Tristan took Mairghread out for walks around the bailey to introduce her to more of the clan and to explain the clan's operations. Sometimes he took her for walks by the loch. On a particularly warm day, she stripped off her shoes and stocking, hoisted her skirts to her knees, and waded in to just above her ankles. Tristan watched, speechless. He'd never seen a lady, any other grown women, do that. She turned to face him with a pure look of innocence on her face. This was just moments before she kicked water all down the front of Tristan's clothes. She laughed so hard she almost lost her balance. Tristan wasn't to be outdone. He marched into the loch, boots and all, and hefted her into his arms. He pretended to be prepared to throw her into the water. She squealed with delight. She encouraged him to do it, stating she was too warm, anyway. It was the first time he had her in his arms since they stood on the battlements together. They shared some dances after the evening meal, but he couldn't hold her as close as he wanted.

On other days, Tristan took Mairghread for rides across the meadow. She asked to exercise Firelight, so Tristan seized the opportunity to spend time with her. It was a chance for him to leave the keep with just his personal guard rather than any of her brothers, who had been constant companions to all their other outings. Since they went some distance outside the castle wall, he took his ten best guardsmen. He convinced the Sinclair men that with ten men to guard Mairghread, there wasn't much that might happen to her. He was certain they understood his meaning—there wasn't much he could do with her. Liam relented, even though his sons stood shoulder to shoulder with their arms crossed as the conversation ended. Tristan thought to himself how he wouldn't want to come across that wall of men on the battlefield. They were a surge engine unto themselves.

Most of these rides involved Mairghread riding Firelight while Tristan rode his war horse, Thunder, but sometimes they rode Thunder together. Tristan explained the massive horse earned his name for the sound he made as a foal when he kicked the sides of his stall. Fully grown, Thunder stood at seventeen hands and was at least two hands taller than Firelight, a horse already considered large. Thunder had a massive head and broad shoulders that carried Tristan to survival and victory frequently.

It was toward the end of Mairghread's first fortnight at Castle Varrich when Tristan decided he would rather share a mount than ride separately. He almost swallowed his tongue the first time they rode out together on Thunder. He stepped into his steed's stall to saddle him while Mairghread waited. She brought an apple for Firelight as an apology for leaving him behind. She said she didn't want him to feel left out or slighted. Tristan laughed and teased her about being so in tune with her horse's feelings, but when Tristan turned around to bring the bridle to Thunder's head, his heart stopped, then lurched forward. It terrified him to see Mairghread's outstretched hand holding an apple for Thunder. The beast liked no one other than Tristan and the senior stable master. He had bitten and kicked many others throughout his life.

Tristan began to drop the bridle to rush forward when Thunder nickered, and Tristan watched him nibble the apple off Mairghread's hand. He watched in awe as she blew into his nostrils, then leaned her cheek onto his massive head. She reached her hand over her head and rubbed Thunder between his eyes. It mesmerized Tristan as his ornery warhorse become gentle as a lamb under Mairghread's ministrations. If Tristan hadn't already been falling in love with Mairghread, seeing her with his horse sealed his fate.

"I canna believe ye could feed him, or that he let ye touch him. He doesnae like anyone."

"Well, he seems to like me well enough. Mayhap he kens ye and I are friends, so he trusts me."

Friends? Friends? Friends!

Tristan didn't want to trust his ears. Is that what she considered them? "Are we just friends, then?" He asked as he placed the bridle over Thunder's head. He looked back over his shoulder and noticed a pretty blush coming to her cheeks.

"Aye. I'd like to think we are. I think we get along well and enjoy each other's company. Isnae that what ye would want from someone ye're considering marrying?"

"So ye think we might become more than friends? Ye still think we might marry?"

"Of course, I do. Dinna ye? It's the reason I'm still here. If I didna still want to get to ken ye or think I might marry ye, I would've asked ma da to take me home."

"I still want to marry ye. I want to vera much, but I wasna sure what ye meant by friends. It sounded like mayhap ye dinna consider me as a future husband."

"I'd rather be friends with ma future husband than enemies or ambivalent."

"Och, aye. Then friends we are."

That day, Tristan walked Thunder out of the stables and helped Mairghread into the saddle. Most of the time, she rode pillion behind him, but he placed her in front of him. When he settled behind her, he realized this would be the sweetest type of torture. Her backside nestled between his thighs, and his arm wrapped around her middle, just below her breasts, causing his cock to twitch and lengthen. He shifted in the saddle to give her some room. The last thing he wanted was to frighten her with his staff rubbing against her back.

After a fortnight of spending afternoons together, both Tristan and Mairghread were almost going out of their minds with unspent desire and lust. They shared many heated looks and found any opportunity to brush their bodies against each other, but they hadn't embraced like they had on the battlements. Mairghread's body ached to hold his against her like it did when they rode Thunder together. Tristan barely hung on to his wits, since he became hard at the mere thought of Mairghread. When his eyes landed on her or he caught a whiff of her fragrance, he almost spilled his seed without even touching her.

It all came to a frenzied head on one of their rides on Thunder. Tristan wrapped his arm around Mairghread as they galloped across the meadow. He drew small circles under her breast with his thumb. Mairghread's inhale pressed her back against his chest, and it pushed her breasts onto his arm, making his reflexes tighten his hold. She melted back into him and tucked her head into his shoulder. He rolled his wrist, so his hand grasped the underside of her breast. She wiggled in the saddle, making her backside rub up against his stiff shaft. Moving with the motion of the horse, Tristan rocked his hips forward, so his cock rubbed between the cheeks of her backside. Her soft moan whispered in his ears when she wriggled again, trying to gain more contact through their clothes. Tristan failed to stifle his own groan as his cock throbbed for release. He turned Thunder toward the tree line and looked over his shoulder to his men. He gave a quick whistle, and the guardsmen reined in some distance from where Tristan halted Thunder. As he helped Mairghread down, he let her body slide along the length of his. They needed no words as their eyes communicated the burning need they could no longer ignore.

Tristan grasped her hand and walked along the trees while making inane comments about them as he pointed to various ones. He attempted to be discreet by leading his men to believe he was showing her the local flora and fauna. He was sure they well knew what was happening, but he hoped to offer some reassurance to Mairghread that they didn't have an audience. He tugged her hand and led her into the trees. Once past a large oak tree, he pulled her into his arms and backed her against the tree trunk. Her arms slid up and around his neck, and she rose on her tiptoes. She met his mouth halfway. The first press of their lips was soft, but within seconds it erupted into a firestorm.

Tristan wrapped one arm around her waist and sifted the fingers of his other hand into the hair above her nape. His tongue pressed along the seam of her lips. It took a moment for Mairghread to realize what he wanted, but once she did, she opened her mouth to his invading tongue. With brief consideration and on instinct, she sucked on it. Tristan growled and dropped his hand to her buttocks. He squeezed hard and pulled up, so she was almost lifted off her feet. She pressed her hips into his and ground her mound against his cock. She was positive there was a length of steel behind his plaid. He had already pushed his sporran out of the way when he pulled her against him, so there was only the material of his *breacan feile* and her kirtle keeping them from touching skin to skin.

Tristan glided his hand down Mairghread's nape to her shoulder and around the front to the ties of her gown. He yanked at them, then caressed down the front to grasp her breast. It fit in his hand as though it were made for him. He was a large man and had large hands, and Mairghread was more endowed than he realized as it filled his hand with his fingers spread open. He squeezed and massaged her breast and her buttocks. She moaned and whimpered as she wanted more but wasn't sure what that was.

"Tristan, please. I dinna ken what's happening to me, but I need ye. Please."

"I ken, little flame. I ken." Tristan leaned forward and licked her exposed nipple. He laved it and swirled his tongue before taking it fully into his mouth and sucking. Mairghread gasped. She'd felt nothing like it before, her breasts full and heavy. She arched her back to press the globe farther into his mouth as his hands traveled to grasp the ends of her skirts. He tugged them up and squeezed her buttocks before lifting her. She wrapped her legs around his waist and rocked against his shaft.

"I need more, Tristan. I ache so badly it hurts, but I dinna ken what to do."

"I shall help ye. I can make the ache go away and bring ye pleasure."

Mairghread looked into Tristan's eyes. There was a mixture of need, confusion, and worry. "Mair, I willna take yer maidenhead until ye're ma wife. But I will make ye mine and mine alone. I'll touch ye where nay other mon ever has, and nay other mon ever will."

With that, Tristan turned and slid his back down the trunk of the tree. When he sat, Mairghread straddled his lap. He squeezed her buttocks again and leaned forward, taking her nipple back into his mouth. His fingers inched toward her hot, wet sheath. He dipped the fingers of one hand into her slick seam. He brought the other hand around to rub his thumb across her pleasure nub. Mairghread's head fell back as she rocked against him. Her moans were almost enough to undo him.

It aroused Tristan further, making the tip of his cock leak. Tristan hadn't been this close to climaxing without a woman touching him since he first realized what a man did with a lass. He was so hard it convinced him he would explode, but he would do nothing about it now. He was introducing Mairghread to passion and pleasure. It was about her and not him. He would either take himself in hand later, as he had been doing at least twice a day since she agreed to stay on, or he would take yet another dunk in the loch when they returned.

For now, Tristan slipped two fingers into Mairghread. She was so tight, and his rod had a mind of its own. It was already imagining itself buried hilt deep. His cock pulsed. Mairghread's body didn't ignore the twitches coming from Tristan's rod, and it almost drove her mad. She reached below her skirts and grasped Tristan's hand. She guided another finger into her.

"Tristan, I need more. I can feel how large yer shaft is. Ma body kens what it will take to feel full. It's yer cock, and if I canna have that, then I need more from yer fingers."

Mairghread surprised Tristan, but it pleased him that she trusted him enough to speak aloud her desires and wants. He didn't want a dead fish for a bed partner. He knew all along Mairghread would be passionate, but he hadn't been sure she would be open to telling him what she wanted. Once again, she amazed him. He could tell from her reactions and her uncertainty that she was untried, so he worried not that she had been with anyone else.

Tristan pressed all four fingers into Mairghread's sheath. He hooked his first two fingers to find the spot just inside her wall and let the other two find the spot just beside her maidenhead. His thumb rubbed against her mons. He'd known enough women during his life to learn just what would please her most. He had a vague vision of other women he'd been intimate with, but now they were all faceless and nameless. All he could see and think of was the beautiful woman in his lap and how he only ever wanted to touch her for the rest of his life.

Mairghread rode Tristan's hand as his other moved up to squeeze her breast. His mouth returned to her free nipple. He sucked as though he was a parched man, trying to squeeze the last drop from a waterskin. A tension was building inside her that she'd never experienced before. It began in her core and spread like a wave rising within her. Her hips took off at their own pace. She had thrown her head back, but now she looked down to observe Tristan. Even with his lips around her breast, he watched her. He felt her sheath contracting around his finger and knew she was close.

Tristan wanted to push Mairghread over the top and let her release crest. He pinched and twisted her nipple and bit her other one with just enough pressure to make her climax. He watched as she bit her lower lip to keep from screaming aloud, but his mumbled name filled his ears. The sight of her climaxing above him for the first time and hearing his name on her lips was enough for him to finish, too. His hot seed shot out as though he were a geyser going off. It seemed like a limitless flow, and it shocked him that bringing her release would be enough to send him over the edge, too. That had never happened before.

As they floated down to earth, Mairghread leaned her head against Tristan's chest and panted. She hadn't understood anything shared between a man and a woman could be so powerful. Magnus never explained what couples experienced afterward, and she never thought to ask. Feelings weren't something her brothers often discussed, even the physical ones. Tristan's heart still pounded beneath her cheek as he removed his hands and ran them along her back in soothing circles. She still clung to his leine as she had throughout their interlude.

"Tristan, is it always like that?" Mairghread whispered. She wasn't sure her voice would come out if she tried to speak any louder. She looked up into his eyes. She dazzled him with the luminescent shade of gray they had turned. He'd discovered after riding fast, her eyes would turn grayer with exertion. They fairly glowed now, and he couldn't tear his gaze away even if he wanted to.

"Nay. It isnae." Tristan saw the look of hurt and felt her withdraw. "Little flame, ye dinna understand me. I meant, it isnae always that good between all couples. It has nae been like that before for me, but I ken it will always be like this for us."

"I hope so." Mairghread smiled and lifted her chin to give Tristan a soft kiss. He eased his hands away, since it was time to return to his horse. He was uncertain how long they were there, but it was long enough to make his men suspicious. He helped her right her gown and straighten her hair. Luckily, she wore it down, so there was no intricate hairstyle to repair.

"Tristan?"

"Aye."

"I wish I'd been able to give ye the pleasure ye gave me." Mairghread looked so serious and almost remorseful that he couldn't help but chuckle. Her brow furrowed, and she appeared not to care for his response.

"Mair, ye did. Ye couldnae feel it because ma plaid was in the way, but I exploded like I never have before. Just touching ye and watching ye was enough to bring me to a release unlike any I've ever had until just now. Truth be told, I felt like a green lad again. Ye'd nae even touched ma cock, and I spilled ma seed."

Tristan and Mairghread emerged from the trees, grinning like the cats that found the cream. They grew serious lest they give away their actions. They mounted Thunder and turned back toward the keep.

Things were progressing smoothly for Tristan and Mairghread, but there was only one thing dampening each other's moods. It came in the form of Sorcha. She hadn't abandoned her belief that she should be the laird's lady and in lieu of that, she should be his leman. On the second night after the Sinclairs agreed to stay, Mairghread sat beside Tristan on his left. The seat for the lady of the keep was vacant, as no one held that position. In deference to tradition, Mairghread slipped into the chair on the other side of Tristan. The meal was enjoyable until Sorcha came to the dais to refill their goblet. While there was room next to the empty chair for Sorcha to stand, she squeezed her way between Tristan's and Mairghread's shoulders. She leaned forward, giving Tristan an unavoidable view of her cleavage, and she pressed her breasts into his shoulder. Tristan looked straight forward and attempted to pay no attention to Sorcha.

Even in only two days, Tristan had already picked up on little responses Mairghread made in different situations. Even though he couldn't hear it or feel it, he knew she sucked in a slight breath when Sorcha came between them. He sensed when her body stiffened as Sorcha leaned against him, and he knew her movement would go unseen, as she wouldn't shift in her seat, but she tensed. Tristan slid his hand beneath the tablecloth and found her thigh, squeezing it gently before leaving it there. He didn't remove it for the rest of dinner.

"*Ma* laird, is there aught I can do for ye. I ken what ye like." Sorcha cooed just above his ear. Her stress on the word "my" was no accident. She intended to show Mairghread she'd already staked a claim and was possessive of Tristan.

"Nay, Sorcha. Ye ken there is naught I want from ye." Tristan bit words out through his clenched teeth. When Sorcha left the dais, he leaned over to Mairghread. "Mair, I'm sorry. I'm vera sorry. Ye ken there's naught happening anymore. Ye ken I've nae touched her since before ye arrived, right?"

"Aye. I ken." Mairghread said no more. Tristan wouldn't ignore that it displeased her. He looked over at Morag, his housekeeper, and waived her over. When she came to the dais, she bent to listen to Tristan's whispered words. They were so low Mairghread couldn't hear everything, but she caught some it.

"Dinna ever let Sorcha serve us again. I want her nay where near Mairghread or me. She hasnae accepted that we are through, and she keeps pressing the issue. I dinna exaggerate that last bit."

"I ken it, ma laird. I watched her with ma own two eyes. That bit of baggage is too big in the breeks by half. I'll be sure she stays in the kitchens where she always belonged. She can serve the lower tables."

"Thank ye." Tristan looked over at Mairghread, who had plastered her serene smile. He witnessed it the night they met, and it meant she felt anything but serene. He'd only known her briefly, but he could already read so much of her. "Mair, I've taken care of it. She willna bother us again."

"Is that what ye think? Ye dinna ken women at all if it is." Mairghread turned her head to speak to her brothers, dismissing Tristan. Just as hurt and frustrated settled into his chest, her hand slipped under the tablecloth and slid over his wrist until her fingers intertwined with those already on her thigh. She gave his hand a squeeze and kept her fingers there. Tristan thought he had found his own little piece of heaven.

CHAPTER 6

*A*fter their time together in the woods, Tristan and Mairghread found any and every opportunity to meet in dark alcoves, under the stairs, outer storerooms, and the battlements to sneak kisses and to run their hands over each other. They were insatiable and frustrated. While the kisses were enough to tie them over, they longed for another chance to be alone. When they returned to the keep after their momentous interlude in the woods, her family was entering the Great Hall. It took one glance for Liam to figure out what they'd been doing. He turned and marched over to Thunder, uncermoniously lifting Mairghread off the horse, and growled at Tristan before storming away. After that, the couple was more careful about their rendezvous.

They were in luck when a messenger arrived from Sinclair lands with an update. Before leaving, Liam gave a directive to his second that he should send a monthly report. As it had taken them almost four days to travel to Mackay lands, and they had been there now almost three sennights, the report was due. Liam and Callum retired to Liam's chamber to review the report. Alexander, Tavish, and Magnus were still in the lists.

The day was sunny and warm, so Mairghread spent the morning in the garden seeing to the vegetables and herbs that needed storing for the coming winter months. She was hot and sticky. Her gown clung to her, and it was making her skin itch. She longed for a dip in the loch to cool off, but that wasn't an option. She was no longer on her own lands where she learned to swim almost as soon as she learned to run. Her clan knew, even at her age, she still liked to go for a dip whenever the weather permitted. As a result, she would alert the guardsmen at the gate where she was going, and she would take a maid, usually Alys, with her. While Alys didn't swim, she didn't mind the walk or the time away from her regular duties. With Alys along, no one ever bothered Mairghread, so she stripped down to nothing. Here on Mackay land, she accepted it would be inappropriate to try something like that. Beyond that, it was close to the midday meal. Tristan had said he would join her.

Mairghread continued to work at weeding the cabbages. It seemed like every time she turned back to the dirt, another weed sprang up in the place of the one she'd just torn out. With a grunt she yanked a tenacious one, pulling so hard that when the roots finally gave, she fell backwards onto her backside. She rained dirt all down the front of herself. An enormous shadow came to rest over her. When she looked up, the sun blinded her, but she would recognize the hulking form anywhere.

"Has ma wood nymph turned into a garden sprite?"

"Nay. There is naught fae aboot me right now. Can ye give me a hand up? I've sprayed dirt down the front of me, and I've got ma skirts in a muddle." Mairghread reached her hand up to Tristan. Rather than take her hand, he grasped her waist and lifted her up to eye level with him. He gave her a quick kiss before putting her back on her feet.

"Yer cheeks are a might pink. Ye're nae overdoing it, are ye?"

"Nay more than I usually do at this time of year, though it is rather hot today. If I were home, I'd go to the loch to cool off."

Tristan's mind raced to an image of Mairghread in nothing but her skin, swimming through his loch. He remembered she was a strong swimmer from stories they shared about their childhoods. There was little they didn't know about each other's childhoods. As soon as the vision entered his mind, he picked up on something else. She still considered Sinclair lands as home. He wondered if she would ever view Mackay lands as home. Looking up at him, she didn't miss the lust in his eyes, and she was certain about what he was picturing. Her mind jumped to him bare as a new bairn at the loch. But just as her mind settled into that fantasy, she noticed a sadness creep into his eyes. It was a flash, but she had seen it. She suspected what might have caused it.

"Ye ken they say home is where ye're from, but home is also where the heart is. I ken that means I can have more than one home. Do ye ken the same?" Mairghread rested her hands over Tristan's heart. A wealth of emotions danced in her eyes, but he wasn't sure how to respond. He wasn't ready to share his feelings because he wasn't even certain what they were, but now he backed himself into a corner. He wanted Mairghread to consider this land and keep as though it were a home with him, and he understood she did, but he was unable, or rather unwilling, to reciprocate her admission.

"I ken." Tristan left it at that. The disappointment in Mairghread's eyes was unavoidable when he didn't offer more. "Would ye like to go to the loch for a swim?"

Mairghread laughed at that. She found it funny that she'd just been ruminating on how she wanted to go for a swim but had accepted it was impossible. "I canna go with ye. It wouldnae be proper. I want to swim, but I will need a maid or one of ma brothers to take me."

"Nay. I'm taking ye." With that Tristan grasped her hand and made for the postern gate.

"Tristan, if ma da finds out ye took me swimming alone, he will flay the skin off yer back. He willna forgive this one."

"He and Callum are going over the report his second sent him. They said they'd be busy for at least two hours. We have time to be back with none of yer kin any the wiser."

Mairghread didn't doubt she was looking disaster in the eye, but she followed Tristan anyway. They made their way out through the postern gate and down to the loch's shore. They'd walked along the shore many times in the last few weeks, so Mairghread was familiar with the area, but Tristan led her farther than they'd ventured before. She realized there was a small cave set in the hillside where the loch curved. She never would have guessed it was there.

"Mair, ye can come in and out of the water here, and nay one will catch sight of ye from anywhere else on the loch. Ye will have some privacy when ye're in the altogether." Tristan smirked at her.

"And what makes ye so sure that I will take any of ma clothes off with ye around?"

"Ye want to go swimming dinna ye? Ye'll sink with all those layers on if ye go in as ye are now."

"That may be, and ye are right that I want to swim, but I willna strip down in front of ye."

"I'll turn ma back and willna turn around until I hear ye in the water. I promise."

Mairghread stared at him for a long moment, "All right."

Tristan heard Mairghread moving about as she took off her clothes. His mind ran rampant with pictures of what she looked like as she removed each layer. His cock throbbed before he even got to her taking off her kirtle. He couldn't keep from shifting his weight from one foot to another, as the wait was agony. What was surely an eternity, but was most likely only a couple of minutes, ended when she splashed into the water. He whirled around and caught a view of a very pale and very toned backside as she surface-dived into the water.

Tristan didn't trust his eyes. Mairghread had stripped down to her altogether. She hadn't even left her chemise on. He yanked his boots and stockings off, then unpinned his *breacan feile* and let it drop to the ground—something he never did since he always took time to pleat his plaid before laying it down. He pulled his leine over his head and ran to the shore. Tristan just entered the water when Mairghread resurfaced. She surprised him by how far she swam from the shore. He made quick work of chasing her. She squealed as she dived back under the water as he came closer. She was slippery as a fish. He was sure he had an ankle, but his hand closed around nothing but water. She came up behind him and splashed water at him. He spun around and dived under the surface. Two could play this game. He knew this loch and had no trouble swimming with his eyes open. She, too, seemed to have no problems swimming with her eyes open as she swam farther down and then below him. They both came up gasping for air, having traded spots.

"Ye are nay longer a wood nymph or a garden sprite. Ye must be part selkie."

"I amnae any of those. I am a lass with four aulder brothers who wouldnae let her play unless she could keep up. I learned to keep up."

"Ye need nae chase me, for I amnae running from ye." Tristan held his arms out to Mairghread as he tread in place. "Come here, Mair."

"Tristan, I dinna think that's a wise choice. I ken I dinna have any clothes on, and I ken ye dinna either."

"Aye. Even more reason for ye to come near. This is the first chance we've had to be alone in over a sennight. Lass, let me hold ye near me."

"We canna go any further than we did in the woods. Do ye promise me that?"

"Mair, I wouldnae dishonor ye like that. I told ye then I willna take yer maidenhead until ye are ma wife. I meant it, and I mean it now."

Mairghread nodded and swam forward. Tristan grasped her hand and pulled her toward him but stopped before their bodies touched. They intertwined their fingers and tread in front of each other. The water was clear enough, so they could make out each other's bodies but not in great detail. This made Mairghread relax a bit, and she smiled.

"Thank ye for bringing me here. I love riding Firelight and walking through the meadow or into the hills on Sinclair land, but I am ma happiest when I can just float in a loch. I find such peace being in the water. I dinna want to leave once I am in." Mairghread leaned back and allowed herself nearly float, mindful that if she laid all the way flat, her breast would bob above the surface. She wasn't daring enough to do that in front of Tristan. As though reading her mind, he wrapped his arm over her belly and pulled her to his side. It forced her to bring her legs up and to lie flat in the water. He leaned forward and brushed a soft kiss against her lips.

"I couldnae wait any longer."

"I dinna ken why ye waited at all." Mairghread righted herself and moved into his embrace. Their legs tangled with each other as they each used one arm to help them stay afloat. Tristan held her close to his body as their lips melded together. There was no way to hide his reaction to her nearness. She gasped as her skin contacted his length of steel jutting out from between his legs. It seemed to search on its own for a resting spot between hers. Tristan floated them back to where he could stand. Once he planted his feet on the loch's bottom, Mairghread wrapped her legs around his waist. The water lapped at her breasts, and her senses heightened by the motion and soothing feel of the water surrounding her. Her hands ran up and down the length of his back before exploring the peaks and valleys of his chests and washboard stomach. The sensation of his muscles rippling beneath her hands made her moan. They looked each other in the eye, never breaking contact. Tristan cradled her bottom in his hands, but this time he didn't massage or squeeze her flesh. He held her as she explored him. Mairghread couldn't reach his backside with her legs wrapped around his waist, so her hands slid up his back and hooked over the top of his shoulders. She leaned her forehead against his to catch her breath. She hadn't realized she was panting.

"Little flame—" Tristan didn't get far before she interrupted him.

"Why do ye call me that? I dinna understand it. 'Mair' makes sense, but why do ye think of fire when ye look at me?"

"Havenae ye ever noticed the color of ye hair when the light hits it? It looks as though flames are jumping out of it. The reds are so bright ye almost canna see the brown. It matches yer spirit. There is a fire in ye drawing me in, and I canna seem to look away."

"I never give much consideration to ma hair. I ken it isnae what most women want. It's flat and straight. Men like women with thick, lustrous hair. I dinna have that."

"Who told ye that? I ken I love yer hair, just as it is. I dinna want it any other way."

Did I just say that I love her hair? Did I use that word? I've never said it aboot any woman before. Now what do I do? I couldnae respond to her feelings earlier, but I can tell her ma feelings on her hair. I ken she noticed.

Tristan held his breath for a moment. He was sure he was right that Mairghread picked up on the use of the word love, but she said nothing.

"Speaking of that fire in ye, why do ye wear so many knives? I never asked ye aboot that after yer first night here. I, along with everyone else, couldnae miss the dirks in yer hands. I realized they came from yer wrists, and ma hand caught the *sgian dubh* strapped to ye thigh when we were in the woods. I even noticed the dagger lying in the side of yer boot as I passed yer clothes on the shore. Ye're mightily well-armed for a lass. Why so many blades?"

"Ye do remember who ma kin is. Ma brothers have always been overprotective of me. Once I turned two-and-ten and filled out, they became adamant that I learn how to protect maself. I'd learned how to wrestle and tussle with them and the other lads when I was a wean, but as we all grew aulder, I wasna allowed to continue. First it was because the lads became stronger than me, and ma da worried I would get hurt. Then it just wasna proper anymore. Since I couldnae wrestle, and ma brothers wouldnae stand for anyone touching me anyway, I had to find another way to protect maself."

Mairghread shrugged, tapping the surface with her fingertips as she remembered several vehement arguments she had with her brothers. Callum and Tavish were the loudest, but Magnus was the most determined.

"Ma brothers didna want anyone to get close enough ever to touch me if I didna want it, so they taught me how to use knives. I can throw them, stab with them, and cut with them. Ma brothers made sure I can come out the winner if I must. Anyway, by the time I was six-and-ten, I'd become good with the knives. Ma brothers nay longer kenned what to do with a sister who was more a woman than a bairn, so they stuck with what they kenned. Each year on ma saint's day, they give me a new dagger. That's how I have one for each wrist, each thigh, and each boot. I've told them I dinna have too many more places I can hide them, so Magnus told me I would have to sew them into ma gowns. Little does he ken I started sewing them into ma arisaids and hems shortly after they started teaching me."

Mairghread grimaced, and her upper lip remained curled in disgust as she continued her tale.

"I had one too many run-ins with Lyle Sinclair, the shepherd's nephew. The boy used to bully me aboot wanting to play with the lads. As we grew aulder, he tried to steal a couple of kisses, but when I refused, he told the other lads I gave them away for free. I put an end to that sharpish. I broke his staff over ma knee and threw one of ma dirks at him when he leaned against a tree. I made sure to let him ken pinning his leine to the trunk was ma intention and nae a miss. Next time ma intention would be to hit him and nae the tree. I didna feel right going out without a dirk after that, but I wasna willing to admit it to ma kin, so I sewed them into ma clothes. I can get to them easily if I need more than what I strap to me, but nay one kens they are there."

"This Lyle Sinclair should count himself lucky I havenae met him. I dinna think I care much for him. Ye keep impressing me, lass. I'd like to watch ye use the blades for something other than threatening ma stepbrother."

"Aye, well, mayhap I can challenge ye later. Whomever throws the best can claim a boon."

"A boon? I dinna think I want to wait that long." Tristan pressed his hand to the middle of Mairghread's back and brought her body flush with his. He kissed the column of her neck from just behind her ear to where it met her shoulder. She tilted her head to give him more space, and he felt the shiver run through her. He nibbled, then licked his way back up to her earlobe. Mairghread tilted her head further and caught his earlobe between her teeth. She sucked, then tugged a little with her teeth. She was sure his shaft grew even harder and longer between them. She hadn't imagined it was possible.

Mairghread reached between them and ran her fingertips over the head of Tristan's cock. How smooth the skin was when it covered something that had surely been forged from iron intrigued her. She let her body slide down his a little so she could wrap her hand around his rod. She'd been peering below the water's surface to glimpse what she touched, but when Tristan groaned, she looked up as squeezed his eyes shut.

"Am I hurting ye?"

Tristan caught the worry in her voice and looked down into her deep blue-gray eyes. He couldn't determine if it was the sunlight, the water's reflection, or just her mood, but her eyes were yet another shade he hadn't seen before. "Nay, lass. Just the opposite. Naught has ever felt as good. I am trying to control maself and nae have this end before it's even begun."

Mairghread smiled at that and returned her attention to her hand below the surface. "I dinna ken what to do," she breathed.

"Aught ye do at this point will feel like heaven. Just slide yer hand up and down but dinna tug or squeeze too hard. That might nae feel so much like heaven."

Mairghread moved her hand up and down. When Tristan thrust his cock in her hand, she was certain she was doing something right. She was so fixated on what she was doing for him, she didn't notice his hand sliding between them. She gasped and moaned when his fingers thrust into her. He didn't test her with one finger at a time like he had the first time. This time, he pressed three fingers into her tight sheath. He almost climaxed, just feeling how she closed around him. He used his thumb to rub her pearl. As she became more and more aroused, her grip tightened. She was careful not to squeeze too hard, but she picked up her pace. Something told her to pump his cock and add a little twist to her wrist. It only took five pumps like this before he was spilling his seed between them.

Mairghread began to lower her legs when she realized Tristan had climaxed, but he'd only just begun with her. He picked up the pace of his ministrations, squeezing her thighs around him. He waded over to a rock in the sun but sheltered from anyone's prying eyes. He laid her back on it and watched as his fingers slid in and out with her juices coating them. He hungered for a taste, blowing on her curls. The cool air against her heated skin made her arch her hips off the rock. He grasped her hip with one hand and slid his shoulder beneath her thighs. Her moans and insensate mumblings continued as she writhed on the rock. When his tongue flicked against her folds, she jerked upwards to catch what he was doing.

"Ye canna be doing that!"

"Aye, I can, and I will. I've dreamed of what ye taste like, and I've wanted to lap up yer honey pot since I watched ye enter ma keep. I will have ma taste and enjoy it." Tristan used one hand to press Mairghread back against the rock, then slid that hand down to cup her breast. He marveled at how well it molded to his hand. His fingers kept slipping in and out of her folds as his tongue flicked her nub. He ran his tongue from top to bottom before dipping it into her. He would lavish more attention to her bottom parts another day. He didn't want to frighten her with these new sensations, so he continued to work his tongue and fingers together until her breaths came in little gasps. He perceived she was almost to the end of her endurance. He brought her to a point where she could almost tolerate no more pleasure without it becoming pain. As she began to spasm around his fingers, he thrust all four fingers into her, sucked hard on her pearl, and twisted and pinched her nipple. The combination of sensations catapulted her to the finish.

"*Tristan!*

Tristan hoisted himself out of the water and wrapped her in his arms. He pulled her onto his lap as her climax ended. She clung to his shoulder as she buried her head into chest. She continued to shake, but he realized it wasn't from the cold. He looked down and noticed tears streaming down her cheeks.

"*Mo ghràidh*, what is it? What's wrong? Did I hurt ye, or do something ye dinna like?" Tristan's heart was breaking to see Mairghread in tears. She looked up at him with droplets still falling down her cheeks, but there was a sense of wonder in them.

"Am I really yer darling? Ye didna do a thing I didna want or didna like. It was just suddenly too much. It was too much for me to feel all at once. I am a wee overwhelmed, I suppose."

"Mairghread, ye are *mo ghràidh* and much, much more. I understand things moved faster than ye might have been ready for. I willna rush ye again, and I'm sorry, *mo ulaidh*. And aye, I do ken ye to be a treasure."

"I didna feel rushed, and it didna move too fast. It was as though time stopped. I just amnae sure how to handle how intense ma feelings are for ye." Mairghread looked away from him and out at the loch. "I dinna think yer feelings are quite what mine are."

Tristan realized Mairghread took his earlier evasion to heart. It had hurt her quite a lot. He didn't doubt she felt like he'd baited her, and then yanked it away. But he didn't want to confess his feelings now for fear she would assume he said what she thought he believed he should say. He also didn't want her to doubt it and wonder if any professions of love were from the afterglow of their lovemaking. He accepted he had to be honest or risk having her retreat from him emotionally and physically.

Mairghread began to lift herself out of Tristan's lap, looking over her shoulder for her clothes. There was no help for it. She would have to put her clothes back on while she was wet as they had brought no drying clothes with them. Tristan tightened his hold on her and stroked her shoulder.

"Mairghread, wait. Dinna get up yet. I want to hold ye for as long as I can. I dinna ken when we'll get time alone again. And I dinna want ye to go until ye listen to me. I choked back in the garden and couldnae admit to ma emotions. I wanted ye to confess yers for me because I needed to ken they are the same as mine. Then when it was ma turn to admit to them, I was too cowardly to risk telling ye. I didna ken how to say it, but I kenned how I felt. How I feel. I dinna want ye wondering if aught I say now is just to please ye or because we shared more intimacies. I will tell ye how I feel, but nae now. I will do it soon, and I will be vera clear to ye. Can ye wait?"

"I dinna suppose I have a choice. I canna and willna force ye to say things ye arenae able to. I amnae going anywhere. Ye ken how I feel. I've told ye, and I think I've shown ye. Just dinna wait too long. I amnae kenned for ma patience. I am many things, but patient is nae always one of them." Mairghread gave Tristan a quick, tight hug, then rose to fetch her clothes. Tristan realized she was so lost in her thoughts, or perhaps in such a rush to leave, that she didn't seem to notice he had an unobstructed view of every glorious inch of her. Tristan rushed to gather his clothes, too. He could feel himself hardening, and he knew if they didn't leave soon, he would lay her back on the rock, and this time he wouldn't stop with just a taste.

CHAPTER 7

As they approached the postern gate, they agreed Mairghread would enter first, and Tristan would follow a few minutes later. If anyone commented, they would say they passed each other near the loch, which wasn't completely a falsehood. Mairghread made her way abovestairs toward her chamber.

"Ye ken he used to take me to the loch. But we never got around to swimming." Mairghread froze. She now recognized that voice, and it belonged to someone she had no desire to speak with. She turned her head toward the sound's direction. "Ye may be what he fancies now. But once he marries ye, it's ma bed he'll be coming back to every night."

Mairghread realized she had nothing to say to the other woman. There was nothing worth saying that would make the woman less hateful, so she took the line of least resistance. She looked at the woman, then turned back to walk to her chamber. Mairghread caught the sound of the feet coming down the hall just before the hand on her arm yanked her around. She looked down at Sorcha's hand on her, then looked up at her nemesis.

Mairghread raised one eyebrow and lifted her chin. She'd been a laird's daughter her entire life, and she played to that now.

"Remove yer hand. I wouldnae touch me again if I were ye. I dinna want ye near me, and I dinna want to speak to ye. I havenae time for yer jealous ranting and hateful words. Leave me be." With that, Mairghread pulled her arm away and turned around. However, Sorcha ignored Mairghread's warning. Once again, she grabbed Mairghread's arm.

"Ye think because ye're a laird's daughter that ye're better than me. Ye think ye're so high and mighty, but ye arenae. Ye're naught but a mouse. Ye havenae even the gumption to speak to me. Ye canna hold the laird's attention for long. He will tire of ye and want a woman who can please him. Yer innocence will be gone in a night, and then yer novelty will wear off. He's been mine for going on two years. If Alan hadnae botched the alliance, Tristan would marry me."

"Ye believe that, dinna ye? Ye're mad as a hatter if ye think that's the case. I'm done with ye now." Once again Mairghread turned away, but Sorcha reached out and grabbed a handful of Mairghread's hair. She yanked as hard as possible so that when Mairghread's neck snapped back, her scream was unpreventable. She turned into Sorcha's grasp and flicked her wrist, pressing her dirk into Sorcha's stomach while using her other arm to reach up and wrap it around the one that held her hair. She pinched the underside of Sorcha's arm as hard as she could, making Sorcha release her hair.

Before either woman did another thing, the sound of running feet came to them. It was more than one set, and they were heavy treads. Mairghread looked up in time to witness Tristan barreling down the hall. Her father and Callum were just behind Tristan. They heard her scream from the Liam's chamber, where they were still working. All three men observed Sorcha's hand in Mairghread's hair.

Before Tristan said anything, Liam pushed past. "What is the meaning of this? Ye dare attack ma daughter?"

Tristan stepped forward to see Liam was just as livid as he'd been when Alan insulted Mairghread. While Tristan didn't think Liam would harm a woman, he was unconvinced, since the situation involved his only daughter.

"Explain yerself woman. What were ye doing assaulting Lady Mairghread?" Tristan demanded.

"I did naught! Lady Mairghread was taunting me and struck me first."

"Sorcha, I wouldnae lie to me or the Sinclair. It willna make things right, and it willna make me go lighter on ye. I ken ye to be lying. I listened to the last of what ye said as I came up the stairs." Tristan turned to Mairghread as she rubbed the back of her head. He pulled her into his arms and checked for any damage Sorcha may have done. "Sorcha, ye should count yerself lucky Lady Mairghread didna snap yer arm or gut ye right here in the passageway. She would have been within her rights. Ye attacked a noblewoman."

"I didna! I tell ye she attacked me first! She was taunting me that she stole ye from me." Sorcha looked at Laird Sinclair as she spewed her next set of lies. Several guardsmen had approached when the scream and sound of running feet reached them. Sorcha counted on the fact that every word carried to them. "She was bragging aboot how the laird's been tupping her every chance he has. She called me a whore."

Laird Sinclair roared as he rushed forward. Sorcha had pushed him to his limits with the Mackays. While he had never struck a woman, this one sorely tempted him. He shook his finger in front of her nose and spoke so harshly spittle formed at his lips. "Ye think anyone here would believe yer vile lies? Everyone kens what ye are. Even I've heard ye are naught but a light skirt. Ye didna think I would hear aboot yer past with the laird? Ye didna think I would hear aboot ye propositioning each of ma sons? Ma daughter is nae a whore, but ye certainly are."

Tristan was losing control of the situation and needed to gain it back. As laird of this keep and with several of his guardsman listening, he had to appear as if he were in command. He'd needed a moment to calm down anyway and to assure himself nothing serious had happened to Mairghread, but it was his turn to talk now.

"Sorcha, I told ye ma reasons for breaking things off. It didna matter who I might marry. I willna bring a prospective bride into this keep while bedding another woman. It isnae yer decision to make. Ye have brought the consequences upon yerself. Ye could've left well enough alone, but nay, ye had to go too far. I release ye from yer work here in the keep. Ye may gather yer belongings, and once ye leave, ye arenae to return. Ye may make yer home in the village with yer kin. If ye would like a croft of yer own, I will arrange it, but I dinna want to lay eyes on ye near the keep again. Ye arenae to enter the walls of the inner bailey without ma permission or that of Alasdair, who's become ma tánaiste. I put up with yer spoiled behavior because ye served a purpose, and I enjoyed ye. Ye have worn out yer welcome. If I discover ye have been near Lady Mairghread again, I'll banish ye. Dinna think for a moment I will ever choose ye over Lady Mairghread, or ye will be disappointed. *Guards!* Escort Sorcha to her chamber and watch as she packs her belongings. Then escort her to her parents' croft in the village."

As the guards escorted her away, Sorcha couldn't leave without having the last word. "Ye ken ye love me. Ye ken once ye've wedded and bedded her and her kin leaves, ye'll be coming back to me. I may nae want ye after dipping yer wick in her. Ye'll be sorry ye didna keep me."

Sorcha's threat lay heavy in the air even as she descended the stairs. Liam looked at Tristan. Mairghread and Tristan held their breath while the anger faded, but disappointment replaced it. They both were sure they wouldn't like what he said next.

"Laird Mackay, I have come to both respect and like ye, but I canna say the same for yer clan. I canna leave ma daughter here with people who try to do her harm. I wouldnae ever forgive maself if I did and something happened to her. She may be a woman now, but she will always be ma wee lassie. I will do any and everything to protect her, so I dinna think a match with ye will work." Liam hadn't failed to notice how Mairghread welcomed Tristan's embrace, or how she leaned into him as he held her close. They had developed a tendre for each other, but he wasn't willing to risk her life for it.

Mairghread looked up at Tristan and placed her hand over his heart. He let her speak. "Da, it isnae the Mackay clan's fault that there are a few rotten people. Ye canna punish them all for the sins of a few. I dinna want to leave here, and I dinna want to leave Tristan. It has been almost three sennights since we arrived, and I want ye to sign the betrothal documents. I willna leave and return to Sinclair land. If ye force me, I willna consent to any other marriage. I willna say any vows but those I will give Tristan."

Liam recognized the defiant and stubborn jut of her chin. While Mairghread might resemble him, her personality was the spitting image of her mother. He'd loved his children's mother more than he ever imagined. He'd never once considered remarrying, nor finding anyone else. When he lost her, he lost a part of himself. He tried to make up for it by pouring his love and attention into his children. Liam knew he wasn't a traditional father, as he openly showed his affection to all his children. He didn't want to break Mairghread's spirit or her heart by denying her this marriage, but the situation frightened him. Two people who held significance to the laird threatened and insulted her twice in three sennights. To him, that was too many in too short a time. He looked at Tristan and had to admit to himself that he witnessed a man who was in love with his daughter. Tristan may not have admitted it to Mairghread or even himself yet, but Liam recognized the countenance of a man who had given his heart away. It was the same one he'd worn whenever he was with his wife, and the same one he had even now when his thoughts returned to her.

After giving Mairghread a quick kiss and explaining where he was going, Tristan left her at her chamber door and hurried to find the guardsmen who escorted Sorcha to the village. The men had gotten an ear full, and Tristan wanted to be sure none would speak out of turn. It would only take one person repeating Sorcha's accusations to ruin Mairghread's reputation. Neither Liam nor Callum mentioned Sorcha's comments about Mairghread's alleged loss of virginity, so Tristan counted on them giving no worth to the accusations. He wasn't so confident about other people. This would make for a juicy piece of gossip that would spread like wildfire. While every clan member Mairghread met seemed to like and respect her, the opportunity to whisper about whether the laird was tupping his potential bride would be too much for many to resist. He would tolerate no gossip about Mairghread, but he was aware there was little to prevent it if he failed get to the guardsmen first.

Tristan left the keep and hurried to the stables. He didn't bother saddling Thunder but led him outside. He mounted his steed and rode him bareback to the village. He caught sight of the men as they were returning and reined in his horse as he approached them.

"Men, I would like a moment of yer time."

"Aye, ma laird. We just left Sorcha with her parents. She was sobbing and spinning a tale any bard would be envious of," said

Hamish. He was one of Tristan's most senior warriors, and Tristan trusted him.

Shite! Just what I didna want!

"Dinna ye worry, ma laird. We set her parents straight sharpish. We didna let her loose tongue flap for long. We pointed out had Sorcha nae behaved so badly, there wouldnae be a reason for ye to send her home in disgrace. We told her mother and father ye banned her from the keep and the inner bailey because of her lies and threats. Her da was ready to take the strap to her, and her mother was beside herself, sobbing that it would disgrace the entire family, her being sent down from the keep. I dinna think her parents were that surprised though. I think they got Sorcha's number long ago." This came from Kyle, a younger guardsman who had proven his loyalty several times over the three short years he'd served Tristan.

"I dinna have to tell ye then the damage it would do to Lady Mairghread's reputation and the Mackays' chance for an alliance and a truce if rumors spread aboot what Sorcha claimed. I havenae compromised Lady Mairghread and never would. I dinna want anyone saying I have. I willna be the one harmed by those comments, and Lady Mairghread has done naught to deserve this. I intend to marry her anyway, but I dinna want our marriage to begin under a cloud of suspicion. It isnae fair to the lass. She hasnae done a thing wrong."

"Aye, ma laird!" A chorus of agreement went up from the group.

"I shouldnae have to say it, but I will. I will ken where the rumors come from if I hear them. If I even catch anyone looking sideways at Lady Mairghread, I will ken one of ye has been telling tales. If that happens, all of ye will clean the privy holes and muck out the moat for the next two moons. Ye will also serve guard duty every night for a sennight. Am I clear?"

"Aye, ma laird!" The chorus went up again.

Tristan spurred his horse on. He didn't want to continue to

the village or visit with Sorcha's family, but he accepted he must. He needed to ensure her parents understood how serious he was about the potential for banishment. Sorcha's family was pure Mackay. Neither her mother nor her father had family in any other clan. If he exiled Sorcha, there were few places for her to go. A woman on her own would be a target for many types of wrongdoers. Sorcha had never been a particularly dutiful servant, and banishment would keep her from being welcomed at any other clan. The best hope she had would be to become a serving wench in a tavern or alehouse somewhere, but more realistically, she would become a whore. That was the roughest life he imagined for a woman. Her looks would fade as she aged fast. She would face mistreatment by her customers and might catch the pox. Tristan didn't want these things to happen to her, and he wanted to hold no ill will toward her, as he had enjoyed his time with her. But he would put Mairghread ahead of Sorcha every day of the week and twice on Sundays, so he held no guilt about his decision.

As Tristan approached Sorcha's family's croft, Sorcha's yelling overflowed from inside. There was no doubt this wouldn't go well. The rantings he heard were all denials of wrongdoings and accusations about Mairghread. Tristan struggled to overcome his anger as it welled inside him. He had maintained his temper while Mairghread was present because he didn't want to frighten her or upset her further, but now he was ready to unleash his rage with a ferocity that almost scared him and would scare anyone within hearing.

Sorcha continued to swear up a storm as Tristan stepped up to the door. Several people stood outside their doors or had stopped work to listen to Sorcha's screams. Tristan was now beyond caring about Sorcha or her feelings. He saw red. He slammed the door to the croft open so hard it hit the wall and swung back toward him. He slammed it against the wall again and held it in place. His massive frame filled the doorway, and he had to stoop and turn sideways a bit to make it through the door.

"*Ye will cease now!*" Tristan bellowed. "I have had more than enough of yer lies and conniving ways. Ye are naught more than a pathetic, jealous shrew. I have never considered ye worth becoming ma wife and nae even ma leman. Ye have always been greedy and reaching. That is why I wouldnae make ye either. It has never had aught to do with Lady Mairghread, or any other woman for that matter. Ye have brought every bit of this on yerself. Ye have naught to blame but yerself. Do ye hear me, woman? Ye have naught to offer this clan. Ye arenae an obedient servant, and I nay longer warm yer bed. Ye are wearing ma good graces thin. I sent ye down from the keep and gave ye the opportunity to make yer home in the village. But what have ye done in the short time ye've been here? Scream like a banshee! I caught what ye were screaming from halfway down the road. I couldnae avoid yer lies in the keep or here, and I willna stand for it. I warn ye now, Sorcha. If ye do even one thing that bothers me, ye will be gone from this clan for good. We have banished nay person from this clan for nigh on one hundred and fifty years. Ye are well on yer way to breaking that. I didna come here to issue ye more warnings. I came to explain the situation to yer parents, but ye've given me nay choice. Ye will have to live with it."

With that, Tristan stormed out of the croft. He looked at the crowd that had gathered.

"I ken ye all listened to every word I spoke. That woman is naught but an angry harpy filled with scorn because she couldnae remember her place. Lady Mairghread has done naught, nae a damn thing, to deserve Sorcha's treatment. Naught of what Sorcha said is true. She is a manipulative bitch. If I learn a single word of hers has been repeated, I will assure the person is lashed."

In the years Tristan had been laird, he had disciplined no one with a whip. He deprived people of privileges or fined them, even put them in the dungeon for short periods of time, but he had not physically disciplined them. The clan members took one glance at Tristan's face, and it convinced them he wasn't exaggerating. They had never imagined it was possible for their laird to be so angry.

Still standing in the passageway, Mairghread pleaded with her father to give Tristan more time to prove he would be a good husband to her.

"I willna say aye or nay. I need to give this some consideration."

Mairghread rushed forward and hugged her father. She knew for such a fierce and proud man, the compromise didn't come easy. She had never once in her life doubted her father's love or his willingness to stake his life for hers. She also understood she would have some work ahead of her to convince him, but luckily for her and for Tristan, she had plenty of experience making her father come around to her way of thinking.

CHAPTER 8

The next sennight kept Mairghread busy with chores and more afternoons spent with Tristan, but she found it impossible not to stop wondering and worrying about her father's decision. He'd insisted upon waiting a moon before he would sign the betrothal, and that time was nearly up. But he hadn't brought up the topic again, and whenever she tried, he scowled at her. She decided another tack was necessary. Since she failed to get her father to talk to her, she showed him she belonged with the Mackays. With Tristan's help, Mairghread assisted with clan issues. She sat with Tristan on days when clan members came to make their petitions, listening to any issues related to women and children. She proved to be reasonable in her decisions. Since she wasn't officially the lady of the keep, she made suggestions to Tristan, and he had the final say. He found her stern when needed, but compassionate, too. The clan soon realized Mairghread had significant experience in these adjudications, and it came out through the course of conversation that after her mother died when Mairghread was two-and-ten, she helped her father with these types of duties. Her father took notice and appeared to be warming to the idea of allowing the betrothal to go forward.

Mairghread also kept busy by helping the laundresses and in the kitchens. She learned to cook from her mother and enjoyed it. Annag welcomed the help. She was getting on in age, and even though she was still spry, she had difficulty standing for long periods of time. Annag took Mairghread's offer to help and put her to work. It took Annag little time to realize what a gem she had found in Mairghread. While Mairghread was more than willing to make the food, just as the older woman said, she took initiative to add extra dishes to the meals and to add extra flavor to various items. The other women in the kitchen found Mairghread easy to work with as she stepped in any time they needed help.

When two of the washerwomen, Bridget and Catriona, came down with the gripe from drinking old milk, Mairghread stepped in to help. At first the women refused to allow her anywhere near the lye soap, but the two missing workers slowed their progress. Mairghread grabbed a cake of soap and walked to the troughs and began scrubbing. By the end of the day, Mairghread had raw hands. The women were worried, and the laird was proud.

Tristan and Mairghread continued their outings whenever possible. The weather turned even though it was still technically summer. Tristan needed to spend more time in the village surveying the crofts, determining what repairs they needed before winter set in. Mairghread accompanied Tristan on these visits. She spoke with the women to discover what the families needed. While the men talked about roofs and tools, Mairghread listened to their genuine needs, such as more grain, more wool, more vegetables, and more meat. The roof repairs began soon after, and Tristan organized several hunts.

While they were in the village, Tristan kept Mairghread as far from Sorcha's croft as possible. She moved out of her parents' home when they would no longer tolerate her sulking and mood swings. Tristan had a rotation of guardsmen who monitored Sorcha in the village. She lived a very lonely existence. She had snubbed many of the women over the years when she flaunted one relationship after another. She had attempted to make too many husbands stray for the women to forgive her. The men of the village kept her at arms' length for fear of how both their women folk and the laird might react.

After one such trip to the village, Tristan and Mairghread set out across the meadow for a late picnic lunch. Mairghread observed the meals she shared with Tristan to learn what dishes he liked best and which he seemed to only eat out of politeness. As a result, the basket contained a heel of bread, soft cheese, cold pheasant, a few thinly sliced pieces of venison, and a jug filled with summer ale.

"Tis quite the feast ye have set out. Tis more than I expected. Ye have been hard at work, and I ken the women appreciate how ye stepped in. I admire all ye've done." Tristan helped Mairghread lay out all the food on the plaid he spread on the ground. They settled in to eat, and it was a few minutes before either spoke.

"Tristan, I'm hopeful ma da is close to agreeing to the betrothal. I dinna want to push him too hard, or he will dig his heels in. But I dinna want to go on like we are if there isnae any hope. I will speak to him before the evening meal."

"I agree. I am becoming impatient with this murky situation. I want to complete the betrothal and post the banns. I ken how I feel aboot ye, and I ken what I want."

"Ye do?" Mairghread held her breath as she looked at Tristan. She'd wanted to tell him she loved him countless times, but after their less than satisfactory exchange that day in the garden and at the loch, she was too afraid to confess her feelings only to find out they were unrequited. Tristan pulled her onto his lap and hugged her to his chest. She rested her ear against his heart, listening to the steady beat. It made her relax. She would gladly spend every moment of the rest of her life in this position and die a contented woman. Tristan leaned back and tipped her chin up for a better view of her face.

"Mair, I love ye. I want nay other in ma life. I canna imagine ye nae becoming ma wife. It's as though I canna remember a time before ye were here. Everything aboot ye fits me just right, and I dinna just mean when I hold ye. Ye impress me day in and day out. I admire and respect ye, and I want to spend the rest of ma life making ye happy. I want to fall asleep with ye in ma arms and awaken to ye still there. I want to ken it's ma seed that grows in yer belly. Ye are the only woman I have ever pictured bearing ma bairns. I canna conceive of any other woman I have ever met that would make a better mother than ye. Mair—"

Mairghread cut him off by kissing him hard. She pushed back on his shoulders until he fell onto the plaid. Once he was lying down, she stretched out on top of him. She showered kisses over his cheeks and jaw and ran her fingers through his hair.

"I canna believe ye feel all this for me. I have said a litany of prayers that ye would feel aboot me the way I feel aboot ye. It is as though ye ken ma inner thoughts, for I would describe ma desires just as ye did yers. Tristan, I love ye with ma whole heart."

Their kiss began gently. It was their best way to share their deep feelings for one another. When Mairghread shifted, and her mound rubbed against his cock, their kiss took on a life of its own. The kiss became heated and demanding. Mairghread flicked her tongue against his lips, then traced them with the tip of hers. Tristan thrust his tongue into her mouth as he thrust his hips into hers. Mairghread sucked on Tristan's tongue, which earned her a groan and two powerful hands gripping her bottom. The hard pebbles that her nipples became rubbed against his chest, pressing through her kirtle and his leine. He groaned again as she arched her back to push them harder into him.

Tristan broke the kiss long enough to scan the surrounding area to ensure they had no audience. His guardsmen, who accompanied them, had fanned out to make a protective circle around the couple, and they faced out. They did this under the guise of surveillance, but everyone recognized it was to give their laird and his lady some privacy. They were far enough away that it was impossible for them to listen to what passed between the couple. The grass was high enough that now that they were lying down, there wasn't much of view for the men, anyway.

Tristan inched up her skirts, so his bare hand massaged her backside. His other hand sneaked between them and undid the laces to her gown. Once he loosened it enough to free her breasts, he rolled them over, so he was on top. Mairghread marveled at the sensations his tongue created on her flesh. She watched as he licked around the edges of her nipple. Then he moved on to the other one and tugged with his teeth.

"Lass, do ye trust me? I promised ye I willna take yer maidenhead, and I still mean to keep that promise. But there are a few more things I'd like to show ye since we're stuck waiting for our wedding."

"Tristan, ye ken I trust ye with ma life and in all things. I want to learn whatever ye can teach me."

With that, Tristan inched down her body until he was kneeling between her legs. He pushed her skirts up for a view of her moist folds. This was the first time he could clearly see her lady bits rather than just touch them. At the loch, the rock was cast in the shadows, making it difficult to glimpse all he wanted.

Now it was a veritable feast for his senses. He caught his breath at the sight of her petals glistening. Her scent was unlike any other's. It smelled sweet, with only a hint of musk. And he was certain this was a honey pot he would want to lick clean. He was amazed and grateful for how ready she already was.

As if Mairghread intuited his thoughts, she remarked, "I seem to always be wet whenever ye are near or I think aboot ye. I dinna ken if this is normal, but it happens every time."

"*Mo ghaol*, it's normal. It means yer body is ready to take mine into ye. It means yer body kens we're meant to join. Until then, it makes it easier for me to pleasure ye in other ways. I have been aching to taste all of ye, and so far, I have had to settle for only some of yer best parts."

Mairghread kept repeating Tristan's endearment of "my love" in her head, but all thoughts scattered when he blew cool air over her curls and heated skin. Next, his hot breath brushed across her folds as his tongue darted out to tap her pleasure button. She gasped for air and half sat up to watch what Tristan was doing. When they were at the loch, she could see no better than Tristan. Magnus had told her men enjoyed doing such things to women, and she understood what he was doing from their first time at the loch. But that still left her unprepared for the sensations that rocketed through her body. Her elbows shook and gave out, so she laid back on the blanket and closed her eyes.

Tristan used his thumbs to spread Mairghread's folds wide and took a deep breath. He was almost dizzy with the amount of air he sucked in through his nose. Even her most intimate parts smelled of lavender and heather. He ran his tongue from top to bottom and up again. This time, he tested the waters a bit when his tongue slid down. He let it inch down toward her most sacred and taboo place. He noticed her breathing hitch, but she didn't stop him. Instead, she let her knees fall even wider apart and lifted her hips off the ground. He drew a finger down the center of her core, coating it with her moisture, and then tapped her tight hole. He wouldn't take it any further than that today. That would have to happen slowly and gradually so as not to frighten her. But he sensed that with her passions as strong as they were and her inquisitive nature, she would try more once they wed. Tristan refocused his attention on her core as he slid three fingers into her to his second knuckle, gliding them in and out. He intended to tease her until she could take no more, continuing the light flicks of his tongue. After a couple of minutes, he sensed she was becoming restless and impatient. He added a fourth finger and thrust them into her. She moaned louder than she ever had before. For a moment he feared he'd been too rough with her, but her gasping words told him otherwise.

"More! I need more. Tristan, please." Mairghread struggled to produce the words she needed. "Oh God, please, Tristan. Ye ken what I want. Please dinna make me wait."

"Shh *mo ghaol*, I will get ye there, but enjoy this time. Enjoy ma fingers deep inside ye. Ken I want naught more than for it to be ma cock. I want to slide into yer sheath and fill ye. I want ye to tighten around ma shaft just as ye do ma fingers."

Tristan returned to his ministrations and continued to move his fingers deep within Mairghread. His tongue swirled around her and her overheated flesh as he reached his other hand up to alternate between breasts. He was sure she was getting close, having already learned the telltale signs of her breathing and how she rocked her hips. It had only taken him two previous lessons to become a star student in pleasuring Mairghread. He slowed and pulled his fingers out almost all the way. She wailed at the loss of contact. He used his thumb to rub her as she became more responsive than ever before.

"I shall make love to ye every day of our lives together. I will bring ye pleasure any way I can. Ma cock is twitching to slide into ye."

"Oh, *mo chridhe*! Tristan, help me. I canna last any longer. I ache so much. It almost hurts I want ye so badly."

Tristan would deny Mairghread no longer. Sliding all four fingers back in to the hilt, he used his thumb to rub her pearl. His thrusts and rubs weren't gentle. Tristan was careful not to tear through her maidenhead, but he offered her all he could. He slid up her body and pressed her breast together, sucking one nipple, then the other while rocking his hips against her. It was all the friction she needed to send her sailing over the top.

When Mairghread was certain she was breathing again, she kissed Tristan and slid her tongue in. She wasn't sure how she felt about being able to taste herself on him, but she longed for the connection.

"*M 'àite an duine. Tha gaol agam ort.*" Ma braw man. I love you.

Tristan was sure his heart doubled in size at Mairghread's words. He was pleased with himself after watching her come apart in his arms. He was sure he couldn't imagine this time together getting any better, but he was soon and pleasantly surprised. Tristan watched as Mairghread floated back to reality, and her chest rose and fell with an even rhythm. She opened her eyes, and her smile was filled with mischief. Before he knew what to expect, she pushed on his shoulders and rolled over on top. Saying nothing or even making a sound, she scooted herself down between his legs. Their roles were reversed.

Tristan assumed she would take him in her hand again, but she had far more in mind. She flipped his plaid back and leaned forward. When her tongue circled the head of his rod, he almost shot off the plaid, unprepared for what she was doing. He may have been willing to introduce her to the pleasures of her flesh, but he never expected her to do as much for him. She looked up at him and grinned.

"How do ye—Ahh" Tristan never finished the question because the only thing he managed was a groan as Mairghread slipped her lips over his cock and took him into her mouth.

This was by far not the first time a woman had pleasured him with her mouth, but it was the singularly most erotic experience of his life. Her eyes had become that luminescent gray again, and her lips were a deep red from their kisses. It riveted him as her lips moved back up his shaft. She flicked her tongue across the top and played with the little hole as he leaked. It took every bit of concentration his brain mustered not to climax at that moment. He watched her as she licked him up and down, then moved her tongue around him. She flicked along the vein on the underside of his rod, and he moaned that time. He had never moaned during love play, but there was no helping it. He desperately wanted her to take him in her mouth again.

Tristan resigned himself to Mairghread teasing him just as he had her. On their own accord, his hips began lifting off the blanket, unable to make them stay still. Mairghread slid her hands over his muscled stomach, up to his chest, running her hands over the smooth skin before sliding them back down to his hips. She grasped them and found that her hands fit perfectly in the grooves along the outside of his buttocks. She lifted onto her knees, so her mouth was above him, making it possible to slide down as far as she managed.

Tristan was a large man everywhere, and all parts of him were proportionate. She struggled to take all of him in, so she wrapped her hand around the base of his cock. She sucked hard and flicked her tongue across the head of his shaft. Then she moved her mouth up and down as her hand followed the rhythm. Tristan recognized there was no holding on any longer. She began a twisting motion with her hand as it glided up and down. He was done for when her other hand cupped his bollocks. He tried to push her shoulders to get her to release him, but she wouldn't budge. He sat up and tried to pull her off. Without looking up, she used both forearms to knock his hands off.

"Uh-uh" Mairghread mumbled.

"I canna come in yer mouth." But the sentence died on Tristan's lips as she wrapped her hand around him again and rubbed just behind his bollocks. He gave in to the pressure and the pleasure, erupting into her mouth. "Mairghread!"

Mairghread lifted her mouth off Tristan and licked her lips, smacking them together. It astonished him that his virgin bride-to-be just took him into her mouth, brought him to climax in a matter of minutes, and let him finish in her mouth. He was pleased. He was shocked. He was confused. And he was becoming angry.

How the bluidy hell does she ken how to do that? I ken from her reaction the first time I touched her nay mon had done that before. But how the bluidy hell did she learn to suck a mon off?

"Before ye go imaging the worst of me, I havenae done that before. Ever. I told ye Magnus explained a great deal to me aboot what happens between a mon and a woman. Just as he told me what a mon can do for a woman, he also explained what a woman can do for a mon. I've been wanting to try this since the first time ye used yer mouth to pleasure me. I just havenae had the opportunity."

"I believe ye. Ye and Magnus have obviously talked aboot a great many things most brothers and sisters dinna. If this was yer first time, and I believe ye that it was, ye are a natural. Did Magnus explain what to do?" Tristan asked the last part but wasn't sure he wanted the answer. It made him ill to imagine her brother may have given her pointers.

"Good God, nay! Magnus never said aught beyond just the mechanics of each act. He never gave me any examples and certainly never gave me any instructions. I just thought aboot how ye used yer tongue on me, and I tried to imagine what would feel good to me if I were a mon."

"*Tha sibh gu dearbh ulaidh.*" You are a treasure indeed.

CHAPTER 9

As the fifth week of the Sinclairs' stay ended, Liam was yet to announce his decision. He'd made up his mind, but he couldn't bring himself to tell Tristan or Mairghread. He kept wanting to observe and reflect just a little more before giving his answer. Finally, he accepted his mind never changed. Instead, what he observed reinforced his decision. He feared what the consequences would be if he made a mistake.

Mairghread's patience was on its very last thread. She was tired of hinting to her father and trying to show him she belonged with the Mackays, that she belonged with Tristan. She was fairly certain what her father's answer was, and it was taking a toll on her temper that he wouldn't just announce it. Tristan took his frustration out in the lists, training harder than he had since his father was alive, and he competed against Alan for the old laird's attention. He fought now like a berserker. He took on two and three men at a time. He was in the lists before any of his men, and he often dragged Alasdair along with him.

"Tristan, ye canna keep going on like this. The men canna keep going with ye like this. Most are too sore or too tired to lift their arms above their waists, and some are nodding off while standing watch. And dinna ye blame them for that. Ye canna keep taking yer frustration over yer betrothal, or lack of one, out on everyone else. Ye may seem calm enough, but ye're a pot that is aboot to boil over."

Alasdair was Tristan's oldest friend. They learned to toddle together and received their first wooden swords together. They were distant cousins, but Alasdair had always been more like a brother than Alan ever was. It was because of their close bond that he dared speak to Tristan so bluntly. It was early morning with the sun just rising. They were alone outside the armory, preparing for the day's training.

"I ken ye speak the truth, but the auld mon willna give an answer. I dinna want to press the issue too much for fear he'll prove as stubborn as Mair warned. I dinna want to give him any reason to say nay. Mair's been trying to get an answer out of him, but she says it is worse than trying to get milk from a bull."

Alasdair snorted. "Aye, a bull. She's right on that one."

"Ma lass is a wise one. I will ask Mairghread to find out if he will meet with us in ma solar after we break our fast. If he's agreeable, then this training session should go easy on everyone. If it doesnae, well, then I will challenge each of his sons. I will make sure they canna raise their arms over their waists either." Tristan and Alasdair spent over an hour going through drills until it was time for Mass. He met Mairghread on the steps of the keep. "*Mo calman*, I'd like to speak with ye and yer da after we break our fast. I canna wait much longer to ken his answer. If I dinna ken aye or nay by noon today, I will kidnap ye and find the closest priest to conduct the ceremony."

"Ye think me to be yer dove? I dinna ken aboot that. I'd imagine most people would say I'm more like a hawk."

"Arenae ye listening to the important part of what I said?"

"I ken what ye said. I also ken there is a perfectly good priest here within the walls. We are walking to Mass now."

"Aye, and Father Peter is a wonderful mon and priest, but I

dinna think he will break with tradition and marry us without posting the banns."

"Canna ye make him? Ye are the laird."

"That I am, but I wouldnae want to put him in that position. I have never wanted to push ma authority onto him, so I couldnae ask him to choose between me and his faith. Besides, I ken I would come out the loser each time."

"Fair enough. I couldnae see maself pressing ye to do that, anyway. I wouldnae respect a priest who ye could so easily sway. I will speak to ma da during the meal."

The morning meal came and went. Tristan waited in his solar for what seemed like half his lifetime. He witnessed Mairghread whispering to her father at the table. He couldn't catch what she said, but he watched them both nod. She smiled at Tristan, and he took that to be a good sign. Now he wasn't so sure anymore. He looked at the bottle of whisky and considered having a hefty tot or two to fortify him, but he didn't want to smell of the drink when his future father-by-marriage walked in. He kept telling himself they would soon be related. Contemplating anything different would put him in a foul mood.

Just as Tristan was about to give up and go looking for Mairghread, a knock came from the door. Tristan took a deep breath, looked one last time at the whisky, and answered. "Come."

Liam opened the door and ushered Mairghread through. Then came her four brawny brothers. Tristan swallowed. He didn't want to have this conversation with an extra four angry Highlanders staring him down. They seemed perpetually angry, even when they were laughing and dancing. He wondered if that was how he came across to others outside of his clan.

Probably. I amnae usually looking to make friends.

"I've come as ye asked. I canna imagine what ye would want to talk to me aboot that ye had to send ma daughter to do the asking." Tristan sensed Liam was testing him.

"I asked yer daughter to speak to ye because it's ma belief this matter involves her as much as it does ye and me." *There, ye cantankerous auld coot.*

"So ye would say."

"I value yer daughter and her opinions. Tis her life, too. I dinna want our life together to start with her feeling overlooked or slighted. I willna do that to her because I dinna consider that to be how ye show love and respect to yer partner." *What do ye think aboot that? How do ye talk that down without sounding like an arse to yer daughter?*

"Backing me into a corner willna serve ye well."

Shite! "That isnae ma intention, Sinclair. I just want to be sure ye ken how I feel aboot Mairghread and how I want our life together to begin."

"Ye dinna feel the need to include her when we were negotiating the contract with Alan."

"Tis the right of it, I admit. I didna ken Mairghread then, and I confess it was more of a business agreement than aught else. But I ken Mairghread now, and I care for her. I dinna want to leave her out of this. She deserves to be here."

"Aye, well, I tend to agree with ye on this. I canna say I agree with ye on everything else."

"Da! Enough of the blathering." Mairghread could take it no longer. "There isnae any reason to go all around the houses. Please just give us yer answer." She looked at each of her brothers and added, "And the lot of ye can keep yer nebs out of it. Ye, in particular, Tavish. I ken ye make the loudest wheest aboot everything."

"I ken I've kept ye two waiting for ma answer. Ye ken I dinna take this decision lightly. When I agreed to betroth Mairghread to Alan, I did so worrying just aboot the clan. I regret that now.

Back then, I hoped peace between our clans would be enough to keep her safe. We've all learned that isnae the case. I willna risk ma daughter. If something happens to her because of the Mackay clan, the truce willna last. I willna stand for it, and neither will our clan. Tis why I havenae given ma answer yet. I ken ye're impatient, but there was much to consider. I needed to see with ma own two eyes that this would be a good fit for Mairghread and both clans. I dinna want any more raids. Neither clan can afford it, and a feud willna serve any of us well. Kenning all of this, I feel I can sign a betrothal agreement."

Mairghread squealed and rushed to her father. Liam held up a hand. "But I still want to wait three moons before ye wed."

Tristan wanted to argue. He had no intention of waiting that long, but he would pick his battles. Mairghread, however, decided this was the time to take a stand.

"Nay, Da. I willna wait that long. I have already stepped into most of the duties of the lady of the keep. Now I am just waiting for the title and the official authority. I will wait one moon. Tis enough time to post the banns for three sennights."

"I willna agree to that. If ye love Tristan as I ken ye do and ye already fit here, waiting two moons will do ye nay harm. That's what I will agree to."

"One and a half moons, Da. Ye dinna want a seven moon grandson, do ye? Make us wait any longer, and that's what ye may just get."

"Mairghread!" Tristan almost chocked on his tongue. He struggled to breathe. He looked at the five Sinclair men and was convinced this was the day he would die. "I canna believe ye just said that. Laird Sinclair, Callum, Tavish, Alexander, Magnus, I havenae compromised Mairghread." He threw his hands in the air in an act of surrender. "I willna. I promised her, and I promise to ye now, she will remain an innocent and intact until the day we wed."

"Ye speak as though I amnae even here anymore. I am a

woman grown, and I ken ma own mind. Ma maidenhead is mine and mine alone to give. I dinna need anyone to make that choice for me. I have made ma choice, Da. I'm prepared to live with the outcomes. Are ye, Da?" Mairghread finished with her fists on her hips. She glared at each man. Her brothers kept shifting their weight from one foot to another. Nothing about a conversation on their sister's virginity made them comfortable. Liam Sinclair looked at Tristan. Tristan looked in part like was he proud of Mairghread, but he also looked horrified.

Poor mon looks like he's aboot to expire. The lass becomes her mother more and more each day. I ken she will do this just to force ma hand. Better to marry her off now as a maiden than later in disgrace.

"Vera well. Ye can wed in six sennights."

With that, Liam welcomed her with open arms. It took aback him how tightly his little girl squeezed.

"Thank ye, Da," Mairghread whispered. "I love ye. I always have, and I always will. I ken ye're trying to do what's best for me. Tristan is what's best." Mairghread rested her cheek on her father's chest, closed her eyes, and sighed.

The next three sennights flew by as Tristan and Mairghread kept themselves so busy they fell into bed, exhausted each night. It helped them to make it to each Sunday when the priest read the banns at Mass. Once the third Sunday passed, both felt like time slowed almost to a stop. Both became impatient again. They had the right to wed now but had three more sennights before the day they would become man and wife.

Now that they were betrothed, they became more open about their fondness for each other. When they began holding hands while walking in the bailey, it surprised no one. They smiled and waved as they watched their laird with a woman who seemed to suit him so well. They liked Mairghread and looked forward to once again having a lady who cared about the clan. One sunny morning, the couple was making their way to the storerooms to check how the stores of grain looked. The autumn harvests would begin in a few weeks, and they needed to check the old grain for weevils before they stored separately it from the new crops. Ainsley, the miller's five-year-old daughter, greeted them just in front of her father's workshop.

"Laird Tristy, are ye gonna marry Lady Margged?" Ainsley's five-year-old vocabulary couldn't quite get either of their names right. "Ye're holding hands. Does that mean ye love her? Will ye be having bairns soon?" The little girl's rapid-fire questions made them both laugh, and Mairghread's cheeks pinkened. Tristan looked at Mairghread, and her pretty blush made his heart speed.

If only it were as simple as holding hands made bairns. I would have had her with child within a week. We would have married over a moon ago.

"Aye, Ainsley. I love Lady Mairghread vera much. We are getting married in a few sennights."

"Ma mama says Laird Sinclair better make sure ye marry sharpish before Lady Margged has a bairn on the wrong side of the blanket. I dinna ken how a bairn can come out on the wrong side of the blanket. I dinna think bairns have blankets."

Mairghread's cheeks were flaming red. She was positive she was radiating heat. She was certain she would scorch anything she came too close to, but she kneeled so she was eye level with Ainsley. "That's just a saying, poppet. I willna be having any bairns so soon. Ye can remind yer mama I must marry Laird Tristan before I can start trying to have a bairn. It doesnae happen the other way around in ma kin. Can ye remember that?"

"Aye, Lady Margged." With that Ainsley turned and ran to her mother, who was hanging out the wash near their croft, which was attached to the workshop. "Mama, Mama! Lady

Margged says she must marry Laird Tristy before she can start getting bairns. Nay one has to worry aboot a bairn's blanket being on the wrong side."

Mairghread was unsure whether she wanted to laugh or cry. Everyone within the bailey most likely heard Ainsley's proclamation. Tristan wrapped his arm around her and kissed her temple. "Ye handled that well. If holding hands makes bairns, then I wonder what kissing can do."

Mairghread swatted at Tristan's chest. She couldn't help but giggle a little. She tried for a serious face. "Ye arenae funny. I dinna want yer clan to wonder if ye're marrying a woman with loose morals. I dinna want anyone considering or saying that it's chicken's blood on the sheet. Mayhap people shouldnae see us spending so much time together."

"Is that what ye really want, little flame? I only want to spend more time with ye."

"Ye're the brawest mon I've ever seen, and I love ye. Of course, I dinna want to spend less time with ye. But mayhap discretion would be best. I donna want to harm yer position by having people gossiping that I'm unchaste. I dinna want anyone wondering if ye're the only mon I've been with."

"Lass, ma clan has gotten to ken ye. They ken the woman ye are. Dinna worry over this. If people considered ye a light skirt, they wouldnae welcome ye in their homes. Ye ken people like to have a wee bit of gossip. This is just something for them to speculate on. Ye'll see, *mo ghràidh*. There is naught to fash aboot."

Mairghread wasn't so sure, but she let the matter rest, as she didn't want this to cause their first argument. Instead, she inched ahead of him and looked over her shoulder. "I'll race ye back to the keep. The loser must fetch the winner a pint of ale and pilfer one of Cook's sweet tarts."

With that, Mairghread took off. She ran around people and hopped over anything in her way. Tristan's footsteps told her he was catching up with her as she weaved through the crowd, her tinkling laughter filling the air. Tristan followed behind, amazed at how fast his intended was. He gave up trying to draw his eyes away from her swaying hips as she jumped over one obstacle after another. He'd almost gained on her when, out of the corner of his eye, he glimpsed a larger boulder tumbling over the side of the wall. He charged forward, attempting to push her out of the way.

"Mairg—!" Tristan's scream died on his lips as he watched in horror as the boulder fell through the air toward her head. Mairghread sensed more than saw something was wrong. She looked to her left and spotted the large rock falling toward her. As she tried to swerve to her right, she became wrapped in her skirts as something rolled under her feet. She didn't have time to glance down or to the side as a crushing weight knocked her to the ground. She landed hard; the air knocked out of her. As she tried to catch her breath, she realized that whatever landed on her was also moving. She craned her neck around to look over her shoulder. Tristan lay on top of her with sweat rolling down his pale face.

"Mair! Are ye well? Are ye hurt? Answer me!"

Mairghread tried to push her shoulders up to wedge some space between her and the ground, but Tristan's weight was too much. "Squashing me," she squeaked.

Tristan rolled off to the side but pulled her along with him. Once she was free of his weight, she sucked in huge, heaving breaths. She looked around, her gaze landing on the boulder that landed just inches from them. In fact, the large rock pinned a corner of Tristan's plaid under it. She looked at Tristan again and burst into sobs.

"Are ye hurt? Will ye nae answer me? Ye're frightening me, little flame."

Trembling, Mairghread shook her head. "I am well, but that boulder just barely missed ye. It could have killed ye. I dinna ken what I would do if ye were harmed saving me." She buried her head in his chest and whispered over and over, "I love ye, I love ye, I love ye."

Tristan's heart swelled with pride and love. It moved him that Mairghread's mind went to him ahead of her own safety, and he felt choked by the depth of love she expressed as she clung to him. He ran his hands over her trembling body to reassure himself she was all right. Once he was sure that she was hale, he shifted their weight and scooped her up. It was only then he noticed the crowd they drew. She burrowed her face in his neck and peppered it with small kisses as she wrapped her arms around it. She didn't look until the crowd applauded. She, too, hadn't noticed the attention they were receiving. Tristan nodded his head and carried her into the keep.

Liam was just running down the stairs as they entered the Great Hall. "What the bluidy hell happened to ma daughter?" he bellowed.

"Da, I'm well. Naught happened to me."

"Tis nae what I heard. What I heard is that a boulder nearly crushed ye. That Tristan saved ye by pushing ye away just in the nick of time."

"Laird Sinclair, I would take Mairghread to her chamber, then speak with you in ma solar."

"Nay." Both men looked at Mairghread after her calm refusal. "Ye willna dump me in ma chamber and leave me there while ye both discuss what happened. I ken someone pushed that boulder, and I ken someone aimed it at me. I amnae dim nor daft. Ye willna send me to ma chamber like a wean."

Both men looked at her, then at each other, then back to her. Tristan changed course and walked to his solar. Once inside, he settled in a chair before the fire. He arranged Mairghread in his lap. He glared at Liam, daring him to object, but Liam nodded. He'd already resigned himself to the knowledge that Tristan now had rights to his daughter and that her affections had shifted from him to her soon-to-be husband.

Mairghread leaned her head against Tristan's broad shoulder and breathed in his scent. His arms wrapped protectively around her calmed her, grounding her enough to sit up and glance between two of the men who loved her most. "Someone doesnae want me here. They dinna want me to marry Tristan."

"Lass, ye canna ken that for sure, but I agree it's mighty suspicious that a boulder should fall from the wall as ye pass. Lad, is there anyone ye can come up with who might want to do ma daughter harm?"

Tristan looked at the older man. It had been years since anyone dared to call him a lad, but he saw only concern and affection for him and Mairghread in the man's eyes. Tristan felt accepted, but at the same time, the weight of the responsibility of caring for and protecting Mairghread became even more real.

"I canna say for sure, but I bet we both ken there are at least two people who would prefer we nae wed."

"Do ye believe yer brother has returned? There's nay way Sorcha has the strength to push that boulder herself. Either way, it had to be a mon, so yer brother or a mon Sorcha convinced to do her bidding. It hurts to ken someone hates me so much they would have me done away with." Mairghread's voice trailed off.

"Lass, I want ye to have at least two guards with ye at all times, along with either one of yer brothers or Tristan or me. Nay, make that three guards. I want all sides of ye protected."

"But, Da—" Mairghread couldn't finish before Tristan interrupted.

"I agree with yer da. I want a mon on all sides of ye if ye leave the Great Hall. Someone is to check any room or chamber before ye enter, and I'm posting a guard outside ye chamber at night."

"So, I'm to be a prisoner even though I didna do aught wrong?"

"*Ye are to be safe!*" Tristan didn't realize he yelled until he noticed the red rise in her cheeks. He leaned forward to kiss her, but she offered him her cheek. "I love ye more than aught, and I will do any and everything to protect ye. Until I ken ye are out of danger, I willna budge on this. Dinna test me on this, Mairghread, because I willna back down."

Mairghread looked long and hard at Tristan and recognized not only anger at the situation and love for her, but fear for her, too. She relented and leaned in for his kiss. It started as a chaste brush of the lips but, as always, soon turned heated. They forgot they weren't alone in the solar. A deep clearing of the throat drew them apart.

Mairghread leaned to whisper in Tristan's ear, "Now we willna have any time alone together." With that, she scooted off his lap and walked over to her father. She leaned over to wrap her arms around her father and kissed his cheek. "I am well, Da, I promise. I love ye, too."

Liam rose from his chair and pulled her into his embrace. He remembered holding her as a bairn when her brothers teased her, or she fell while chasing after them. He remembered the little girl she was as he held the woman she had become.

CHAPTER 10

Over the next couple days, Mairghread settled into yet another routine as guards and her brothers or Tristan followed her. She resented the inconvenience of having to ensure there were always four warriors with her. It was only the knowledge they did it out of love that kept her from losing her temper. Along with the guards came the restriction that they didn't permit her to leave the castle walls. She wasn't to travel to the village, and they discouraged her from even going outside. By the third day, Mairghread was getting restless. She'd done all the sewing she had, which included finishing her wedding dress. She'd checked the inventory and reviewed the accounts twice. She assisted with all the meals and even helped the servants change the linens in the chambers. She was bored. For her, boredom led to mischief. She began making the beds in such a manner that her brothers and Tristan couldn't crawl under the sheets without ripping the sheets or pulling the bedding apart. She hid her father's leines and spare plaids.

After a week of tricks and pranks, Tristan relented. "*Mo chridhe*, I ken ye're bored and frustrated. What say ye we go for a ride and then have a picnic outside the walls today? I will take ye to our spot at the loch."

"Tristan, can we really? Och aye, please."

"Aye, vera well. Go put on yer riding boots and meet me in the bailey."

Mairghread wrapped her arms around Tristan's neck and stood on her tiptoes but was still only able to brush her lips against his chin. "Thank ye, *mo chridhe*. I will be ready in just a moment." With that, she bounded up the stairs, taking two at a time.

There was no helping Tristan as he watched her with a smile and a shake his head.

Lovesick fool, I am. I'd do aught to make that lass happy.

Tristan stopped by to the kitchens to pick up the picnic basket he requested and moved out to the stables to retrieve their horses, which he had already ordered saddled. It seemed like only seconds later that Mairghread appeared with her hair tied back and arisaid wrapped around her. They mounted and headed toward the gates. Mairghread looked behind, and it shocked her that they seemed to leave the keep alone. Her eyes looked around the bailey, then scanned the horizon in front of her.

"Aye, we are alone for today. I willna take ye far from the keep but just far enough to have some privacy."

"Tristan, ye're sure it's safe for us to do this?"

"I wouldnae bring yer out here if I didna ken I can protect ye."

"Nay, it isnae that I think ye canna protect me. I ken ye can better than anyone else. I dinna want to tempt fate though." Mairghread shivered, even though the breeze was light and warm. Something didn't seem right about leaving the keep after all the effort Tristan and her family put forth over the past week to keep her inside the walls and well-guarded. She didn't know how to describe it, but she had a sense something wasn't as it seemed or as it should be. They trotted for several minutes. Then she reined in.

"Tristan, I dinna want to go out after all. Nae without guards. If something goes wrong, I dinna want ye harmed or killed because ye alone are guarding me. Please, will ye either take me back or have guards follow us?"

What he was hearing stunned Tristan. After a week of Mairghread's mischief and attempts to evade her guards, now that he was giving her the opportunity for the freedom she clearly craved, she didn't want to go. His frustration was mounting, but as he looked at her and watched her eyes constantly scanning the horizon, he sensed her building fear. It was almost a panic.

"*Mo chridhe*, if guards would make ye feel better, then I shall have some join us. Wait here." Tristan spun his horse around and cantered back to the gates. Just as he entered the bailey, all hell broke loose. Mairghread was unprepared for her horse jolting beneath her, then seeming to slip from under her. She screamed as she looked down at the arrow protruding from her horse's flank. Firelight began to fall, so she pulled loose of the stirrup to tumble clear of the heavy animal. She looked up as she fell backwards, and she watched more arrows fly overhead as they soared toward the men on the battlements surveying the surrounding area. She landed hard on her back, and all the air whooshed from her lungs. Before she understood they were being attacked, three horsemen galloped toward her. She tried to roll over and scramble to her feet, but she still struggled to draw a full breath. One man leaned forward and grabbed her around the waist, pulling her across his lap. The other two men rode at his sides. All three used their targes to protect them from the arrows now raining down from the battlements.

"Nay! Ye might hit her!" Mairghread didn't miss Tristan's bellow from behind her. She saw him giving chase but could do nothing to pry loose from her captor. She watched galloping hooves eat up the ground, and she realized if she broke loose, the horses would trample her in the fall. She couldn't get away by trying to remove the man's hold on her. Instead, she threw her leg over the side of the horse to sit astride. Her movement distracted her captor long enough for her to draw the *sgian dubh* from her boot.

With little forethought, Mairghread twisted her head to peek over her shoulder as she drew her arm up. Not so much as a second thought crossed her mind as she plunged the knife into the neck of the man who held her. He bellowed and released her to grab the knife from his neck. She threw her head back as hard as she could and smashed it into his face. His grip loosened on the reins, and she seized the opportunity to twist as much as possible to push him from the horse. He lurched sideways and toppled. He grabbed onto her skirts as he went. However, her attacker's foot was stuck in the stirrup, so he didn't fall clear of the horse. Rather, he was being dragged along the ground.

Mairghread risked being pulled off the horse, too, as the man still had a hold of her skirts. She brought her foot down as hard as she could on his wrist, breaking his grasp. She righted herself on the horse and grabbed what she could of the reins. The horse continued to gallop, despite all the movement on its back. The fight spooked it, and it seemed to have no intention of stopping, despite Mairghread pulling on the reins. The other two men pulled ahead during the scuffle, but the one on the left looked back to check on his companions. His startled expression morphed into rage. Mairghread gasped when she recognized the man's face.

"Alan."

"Aye, ye wee bitch. They promised ye to me, and I shall have ye." Alan slowed his horse and allowed Mairghread's frightened steed to catch up. He reached out and grabbed her around the waist, yanking her onto his horse. Once she was in his lap, he released her waist and grabbed a handful of her hair. He wrenched it back, and she squealed. "That is a sound I will get used to as I plow ye morning, noon, and night."

Alan grunted near Mairghread's ear. He released her hair, and his hand traveled down to grab one of her firm breasts. She was certain she would be ill. An entirely different sort of fear settled into her stomach as they approached the woods. He squeezed hard over and over, and when his thumb found her nipple underneath the fabric of her gown, he pinched mercilessly. She leaned forward and sank her teeth into his arm. She tasted blood before her head snapped back from him pulling her hair again. "I will kill ye once I am bored with tupping ye. Perhaps I will kill ye while I tup ye. I might just strangle the life out of ye."

"Ye may well do that, but yer brother will kill ye for even considering touching me, let alone what ye might get away with."

"Ma brother has to find me first." Alan laughed into her ear as his hand slid down the front of her gown and grasped her mound. He tried to dig his fingers in, but the many folds of her gown kept him from succeeding. Mairghread wasn't sure if she wanted to die now or die trying to kill him herself.

Mairghread looked around as she tried to gain her bearings. She wasn't familiar with the stretch of land they traveled. It was farther from the keep than she ever traveled with Tristan. She recalled Tristan telling her that Beatris and Alan would travel some of the same route to Clan MacDonnell as she and her family would travel to return to Castle Dunbeath. They weren't yet on that path, so she couldn't imagine where they were going. She glanced at the sun, trying to orient herself. She knew the sun was nearly to its zenith, so she figured they headed west instead of southeast. She assumed Alan was trying to confuse Tristan and her family. She didn't doubt they would chase after her, but the three times she attempted to look back garnered her breast an excruciating squeeze from Alan's meaty paw.

"Dinna bother," Alan taunted. "He has nay more idea where I'm taking ye than ye do. But I shall enjoy our destination since I will strip ye bare and pump ma cock in ye just like I said I have the right to all those sennights ago. Tell me, has Tristan broken ye in? Or are ye still a wild filly needing a fat cock to train ye?"

"Ye'll be dead and cockless before ye ever couple with me," Mairghread threatened.

"Couple? I intend to fuck ye, ma sweet."

Mairghread wanted to retch at the horrid endearment. She considered whether she should, since Alan's tight hold around her middle and the jarring hoofbeats, coupled with her fear, made her want to vomit. The gorge rose in her throat until she could no longer resist the need to cast up her accounts. It spewed forth, all down Alan's right leg and boot. When the strange consistency splattered the horse's flank, the animal stumbled and whinnied.

"Cease!" Alan roared, to which Mairghread suffered another round, the smell weakening her stomach all over again. She wiped her mouth against her sleeve near her shoulder. She felt dizzy and terrified, a combination that made it difficult for her to think. She forced deep inhales through her nose as she once again looked around. She'd felt the horse's direction shift while she leaned over, and now she estimated they headed south, as she had expected.

Mairghread knew she still had her knives, so, as long as Alan didn't strip her of her clothes, he wouldn't find them. She couldn't move her wrists to flick the ones in the bracers loose, but neither did she want to remind Alan that she kept them there. She feared them being used against her if Alan realized they were so easy for him to reach. She closed her eyes and pictured Tristan coming for her. It settled her terror enough for her to look toward the other man who rode with them. She thought she recognized him, but she wasn't certain. She'd met most of Tristan's warriors, but she couldn't keep all their names and faces straight yet. She glanced down and was certain she'd met him when she recognized not only the Mackay plaid the man wore but the scar on the outside of his right calf. The man had stitches when Mairghread first arrived. She'd helped remove them. She raised her eyes and glared at the man, but his unrepentant smile made her hiss and spit.

"A wee hellion. I told ye I like ma women with some fight. But anger ma mon, and I willna stop him from beating ye or taking his turn." Alan rocked his hips forward, pressing his arousal against Mairghread's backside. "After mine, of course."

It tempted Mairghread to change her plans and reach for her blades while headbutting Alan, but they entered a forest, and it would only endanger her more to try to fight. She would have to wait for a better opportunity. And she was determined she would find one.

Tristan roared with rage. He recognized the three men. He was convinced the one on the brown mare was his stepbrother without seeing his face. The other two were guardsmen he thought were loyal to him. He gave chase as fast as his stallion could carry him. They had only a small head start as he and Mairghread hadn't gotten far from the gate when she asked for the guards.

How had she kenned? How could she have possibly predicted this unless she kenned it was to come? Has she been playing me for a fool? Nay! Nay! Nay!

Tristan's mind ran away from him as his thoughts raced into dangerous ground. He watched as Mairghread struggled against her captor, and he was both shocked and proud when she plunged the knife into the man's neck. But in the next moment, his heart nearly stopped as he watched the man almost drag her from the saddle as he fell. He spurred his horse just as Alan turned around. Tristan had an unobstructed view of Alan's face now. He would kill him. Tristan's heart almost beat out of his chest as Alan grabbed Mairghread. It was no consolation to know who had her. He didn't trust Alan not to abuse her or kill her.

Tristan was only vaguely aware of the men riding alongside him and behind him. Mairghread's brothers had been in the practice yard when the cry went up. They ran to the stables and grabbed their horses without saddling them. All four rode bareback as though they had been born on a horse. A score of guardsmen were following behind as they took time to saddle their horses. Twenty-five men chased after Alan, Mairghread, and the traitorous guardsman.

Tristan knew Alan headed west to try to confuse him. He wasn't certain where Alan intended to go, but he knew why he continued away from the keep. He pushed Thunder to keep Mairghread and Alan, along with his treasonous guard, in sight as they rode over hill and dale. He struggled to see how Mairghread faired. As best he could tell, once he'd seen her vomit twice, she remained still. He could only imagine the threats and vile notions Alan spewed at her. He admired that she wasn't panicking, but he also wondered if she were too petrified to put up any more fight. He reminded himself that Mairghread was intelligent and a strategist. He grew certain she was planning her moves and wouldn't act rashly and waste any chance she gained to break free.

Once the posse reached the woods, they fanned out as they entered. It was the only way for so many horses to make their way through the densely packed undergrowth and not fall too far behind. After almost an hour of slow progress, Tristan raised his fist, and all the men came to an abrupt stop. He strained to hear any sounds not from nature. He listened for the sound of hooves, the sound of labored breathing, cries, or voices, but there was nothing. Not even the birds chirped or the squirrels ran. It was deathly silent.

The men looked at each other. Where could two horses go and not make any noise at all? Tristan dismounted and scanned the forest floor. The other men did the same as they looked for any evidence of tracks or disturbance. They inched along as they all tried to determine the best route to follow. It seemed like an eternity to Tristan, but it had to be less than another half an hour before a bird call carried on the wind. It was quiet and muffled. The four brothers moved as one as they left their mounts behind and stalked toward the bird call's direction. Tristan recognized it, too. Mairghread taught him all the bird calls she and her brothers used when they were children and some the men continued to use. The call they all recognized was a warning of danger.

Alexander gave a responding call, but nothing came back. They continued to move forward and were creeping along when another call came, but it seemed to come from behind them, almost in the direction they came from. Tristan and the Sinclair men looked at each other and shook their heads. They turned back to look at the men they left behind them. Many were looking around, just as baffled by the sound. A third call came from the left, then the sound of splashing. Tristan pointed, and all the men surged forward. Some still on horseback and others leading their horses on foot.

Alan and the remaining man with him separated shortly after entering the woods. Alan dragged Mairghread from his horse and tossed the reins to the Mackay warrior. The other man took both horses with him as Alan forced Mairghread to proceed on foot. Alan barked, "Confuse them."

Mairghread strained to see if she could make out Tristan or

her brothers, but the trees were too densely packed. She heard rushing water and dreaded facing a fast-moving river. She wondered why Alan wouldn't have them ford the waterway on horseback, but she realized he wanted their pursuers—here rescuers—to lose their tracks. She stumbled several times as she tried to keep up with Alan's near jogging pace when he wouldn't let her pick up her skirts. They became wrapped around her legs, slowing them both.

"Let me hold ma skirts, or I canna keep up," Mairghread panted as the dirk of Alan's dirk bit into her neck. She'd considered using her tangled skirts to her advantage, but she feared Alan dislocating her arm from her shoulder or dragging her by the hair. Or worse, slitting her throat. Her eyes scanned their surroundings, constantly searching for any sign that rescue was approaching or a means to escape. She caught sight of several trees she could scale if she could break free and make a dash for them, but she suspected Alan would climb just as well as she could. If she could lose him long enough for him to not spy in which tree she hid, she would wait for Tristan and the others or until nightfall.

The sound of horses and men reached them, and Mairghread was certain it was Tristan giving an order and her brothers talking. Alan must have heard it too because he covered her mouth with his hand. She decided to risk the dirk and went limp in Alan's arms. She managed to make two bird calls before Alan slammed his fist into her eye. She also caught two responding calls but coming from different directions. One sounded like Alexander, but the other wasn't quite a match. She wondered if it was Alan's man trying to throw off the search party. She recalled Alan directed him to confuse her rescuers. She didn't doubt her brothers knew which were her calls and which were an imposter's. She prayed Tristan listened to her brothers, even though she believed they were still on his land.

She stifled a scream after Alan punched her as she was

certain screaming would only incite him to more violence. The menace in his eyes was nearly maniacal. She'd never such hatred and wildness in one set of eyes. She wondered if he feared Tristan and the others were drawing too close. She would keep making bird calls if she could, but she wouldn't outright defy Alan for fear her life would be forfeit right then and there. Mairghread didn't trust him for a second to keep her safe, and she believed that as much as he desired her, he would have no qualms killing her if she became too much of a problem. He hefted her over his shoulder and poked the tip of his blade against her ribs until the reached the river shore.

"In," Alan hissed as he pushed her in front of him and down the riverbank to the rushing water. She tried to hold her skirts up, but the first step took her mid-calf deep, and the next to her knees.

"It's too fast and too deep. I canna cross without being swept away."

"I didna ask for yer opinion. I gave ye an order." Alan stepped past her and nearly sank to his waist. If Mairghread weren't so frightened for her life, she would have laughed and said, 'I told ye so.' But she understood that would get her nowhere but likely drowned. Alan regained his balance and pulled her along, his fingers biting into her upper arm.

Mairghread tried to keep up with Alan's longer stride, but the weight of her dress slowed her. The current dragged at her skirts and pushed at her legs. She raised her other hand to try to keep her balance, but she did so without thinking and lost hold of the material. Two more steps brought the water over her knees, but Alan continued to trudge through, his height an advantage. Her legs weren't long enough to tread through the fast current. She stumbled over a rock and pitched forward. She landed with a splash and tried to kick to keep afloat.

"Get up, ye lazy tart," Alan demanded. He hauled her back

onto her feet and shook her. He swayed as the current nearly overcame him.

"I'm trying, but ye arenae the one with skirts that now weigh a ton. I canna cross with ye tugging."

"And I amnae letting ye go, so make do." Alan swung Mairghread in front of him, yanking her arm behind her back. His other hand grabbed a fistful of hair as he shoved her once more. He tugged so hard that her neck snapped back when she attempted another bird call. "If ye dinna want to drown, then shut yer gob."

She knew, even with the swift moving water, she would survive swimming if she weren't trapped in her kirtle. She'd grown up swimming in the North Sea's rough currents, and this reminded her of accepting senseless dares from her brothers. She tried to nod her agreement, but Alan's hold was too tight. She led the way until he once more became impatient.

"Useless," he snarled as he took another step. Neither could have predicted that the water would suddenly rise to Alan's chest, or rather that he would sink. The current caught her and pulled her loose from Alan's grip. As she fought to roll over onto her back and float, she spotted moss growing on the trunk of a tree on the bank. As she floated past, she got her bearings and whistled again, trying to tell the searchers to move east.

She lifted her head to keep her nose and mouth out of the spray. She looked for Alan but didn't see him at first. Then she caught sight of his blond hair bobbing above the water then disappearing. She couldn't tell if he was swimming toward her and keeping his head down except to breathe or if he couldn't swim at all. She felt the water change course, so she struggled to roll back onto her stomach to see where she was going. She tugged at her skirts, battling to pry her legs free. The water spun her so that suddenly she was floating on her back once more, but her feet were leading.

"Mairghread," Alan spluttered. She tried to look back,

disliking how close his voice was to her suddenly. She refused to accept that she would drown or that he would catch her. She would call to her brothers again. This time, she whistled over and over as she tried to keep her head above water. She couldn't hear any return calls over the booming sounds that water made around her ears. She wondered if it swallowed her calls or if anyone heard her, and she simply couldn't hear them.

Her dress was proving to be an even greater threat than Alan. It snagged on a rock and dragged her under until she pulled it loose. It caught branches, pulling them toward her head. She fought to shake them free. If she didn't lose the weight of her gown, she would be unable to prevent herself from drowning. It scared her to stand upright to test the depth for fear the heavy fabric would pull her under. She sensed while the river wasn't terribly deep, it was still deeper than her own height. She reached down to the waist of her kirtle, searching for the dirk she kept hidden in the folds of the gown.

Mairghread slid it free, her fingernails biting into her palm as she encircled the hilt and clutched it as tight as she could. The water tried to pry it free, but she was determined not to lose it or any of her other dirks. She began cutting the laces on the front of her gown. It terrified her that she would inadvertently stab herself, but she had little choice. She couldn't do two things at once: cut her laces and watch where she was going. She figured where she was going wouldn't matter if she sank in the process and never returned to the surface. She focused on placing her knife carefully under the strings and sawed through them.

She was so intent on her purpose that she didn't see the massive tree limb sticking into the water until her feet jammed into it. She howled as the jarring sensation rattled through her bones. She grabbed onto the tree branch and pulled herself into the vee of two branches. She was able to wedge herself in and stay, despite the swift current. She continued sawing through the laces of her dress until they gave way. She tried to shrug out of the wet material, but it was attached to her like a second skin. Mairghread whimpered in frustration. She reached down to just above her knees and stabbed her knife into the material. It gave way, and the knife almost traveled through the material into her leg. She cut through the fabric as far to one side as she could reach, then cut along the other side. Once she managed this, she tucked the knife back into its sheath and reached for the fabric now dangling around her legs. She pulled her legs through the large hole she made and tried to rip away the cloth to be free of its cumbersome length, but she struggled to do it in the water. She whistled again as she looked around. The rushing water around her head still kept her from being able to hear anything else. She wondered if anyone heard her whistle. The answer to her question came in the way of a most unwelcome response.

"Ye hoped ye were free. I see ye have done some altering to yer gown. All the easier for me to get between ye thighs, *mo chaileag*." Mairghread wasn't Alan's sweet anything. She glared at him as he approached the riverbank across from her. She hadn't seen him leave the water. He'd made his way to the far side of the river and climbed out. Now he inched back down the embankment, but when his feet hit the water, he paused.

"Come to me now, and I willna punish ye over much. Make me come for ye, and I will beat ye within an inch of yer life." Alan held out his hand to Mairghread and wiggled his fingers. She looked at them, then at the flowing river. She took no time at all to consider her options: go to him and the hell he offered, attempt to swim away, or drown trying to escape. The only one she wasn't willing to consider was the first.

As the seconds ticked away, she watched his frustration grow. His toes were in the water, but he hesitated to advance. He continued to reach for her, but he would never would since she was nearly across the river from him. She wondered why he didn't come in after her, but she wouldn't ask. She didn't care enough to know. She would use it to her advantage.

She released her hold of the tree and pushed off. She ducked under the branch and swam away. A hard tug snagged her dress, and she struggled to break free. She feared he was quicker than her and gotten a hold of her gown. As she twisted to break free, she realized it was the tree holding onto her gown. In what seemed like a cruel twist of fate, the tree that allowed her the chance to free herself of her gown was now what held her gown captive.

Rage simmered within Mairghread as her chest burned with the need to breath. She was fed up with being held against her will. She grabbed onto the farthest part of the submerged tree limb within her reach and pulled herself toward it as she kicked as hard as her legs allowed. Suddenly, she shot through the water and almost hit her head on the limb as the fabric gave way. She felt lighter, and her legs were free to propel her. When her head popped above the surface, she gasped a large breath before letting the water press down on her. She swam with the current as it pushed her further downstream, staying underwater for as long as her breath lasted, but her lungs screamed at her to come up for air again. She surfaced and gulped as much air as her burning lungs could stand. Mairghread looked around her. There was no one in sight. Not even Alan.

Mairghread looked and tried to judge just how far she traveled underwater. She recognized nothing on either side of the river. She floated on her back again as she looked in the direction from which she came, but there was no sign of Alan anywhere. She whistled once again, but she was no longer sure which direction the river flowed. When nothing stirred, she rolled back onto her stomach and swam to the shore. She pulled herself from the river and lay panting.

I shall close ma eyes for just a moment to catch ma breath.

The world went black around her.

"That whistle means she is to the east," Callum called out. He switched directions, and the search party followed him. It was leading them to the sounds of a fast-moving river. As they approached the bank, two sets of footprints were visible. One was large and sunken farther into the mud, and the other was smaller and sat higher in the mud.

"It's them." Alexander looked across the river before plunging in without another word. He made quick work of crossing the churning water and climbed onto the far bank. He followed the river about ten yards. "There is only one set of prints over here."

Tristan scanned the far bank and the land further past it. There was nothing and no one there. He looked down river and thought he saw something in the water. It looked to be brown and floating on the surface. His heart lurched as he worried it might be hair. He shaded his eyes and squinted, but still couldn't tell what he saw.

"There! Down river! There!" Tristan pointed and ran along the riverbank toward what was becoming recognizably hair. Short hair. Alexander moved parallel to the group, and they all stopped short when they spotted a man floating face down in the river. Alexander jumped back into the river and waded over to the body. He grabbed the man's shoulders and turned him over. Alan's face starred back at them with open and unseeing eyes. His blond hair had darkened once it was wet and was plastered to his face and neck. Alexander pulled him to the bank, where everyone else waited.

"He couldnae swim even though I tried to teach him several times. Why would he enter the river in such a deep spot, kenning he couldnae swim?" Tristan's eyes searched the shoreline on both sides for some hint of where Mairghread might be. Alan wouldn't have intentionally let her get that far. Perhaps he entered the water to go after her. Tristan feared the current had swept away Mairghread. As he began to turn back toward his men to tell them to fan out along the river, he noticed something stuck on the tree limb even farther down the river. He rushed toward it and recognized the fabric caught on the tree. He waded into the river to pull the material free.

Tristan trudged out of the river and returned to the Sinclair brothers, who stared down at Alan's dead body with varying degrees of hate and loathing. Tristan examined the material. It had once been the skirt of Mairghread's kirtle. Something tore part of it cleanly away, but something else made a jagged tear in another part. Tristan knew Mairghread kept more than one knife on her, so the one lodged in the dead guardsman wasn't her only weapon.

She must have cut away her gown, so she could swim free.

Tristan whistled, and Thunder emerged from the forest. His faithful steed hadn't been easy to train as a colt, but the horse now responded like an extension of himself. He mounted and held out the fabric. "She's torn off her skirts to make it possible to swim away. She must be further downstream. Angus and Seamus strap Alan to a horse and ride double. We take him to his mother." He kicked Thunder's flanks and took off as the others mounted behind him and followed.

On horseback, they made quick progress along the riverbank. Tristan came across a spot where something had disturbed the mud. He dismounted and looked around. Mairghread left her arisaid behind when she fell from her horse outside the gates, and now she had only part of her kirtle left. Tristan worried she would become ill with little clothing and being soaking wet. His urgency to find her bordered on hysteria. He forced himself to slow down and breathe as he looked at the mud. Magnus came alongside him, his brow furrowed as he looked down and took a tentative step forward. He gazed at the mud and squatted for a closer examination.

"Notice the pattern in the mud. It shows where someone was lying, but then someone or something dragged them up the embankment. The imprint of the body is the right size for Mairghread, but who would have dragged her away?" Magnus wondered.

All the men scanned the surrounding area. There were small boot prints at the top of the rise and two other sets of prints. One was larger and clearly made from a boot, and one the same size as the first, except the second set of smaller ones wasn't made by boots but bare feet. However, all three sets seemed to just disappear once they were at the top of the riverbank. There was no more to guide the search party.

"Barefoot? No one lives around here that I ken of," Tristan mused. "Why would anyone be barefoot? We havenae had any reports of any lawless men in these parts. Is it possible that Mairghread lost her boots in the river?" Tristan glanced back at the water. "I think it is. We are almost on the boundary with MacDonnell lands."

"MacDonnell? Isnae that where ye sent Alan and Lady Beatris?" Callum asked.

"Aye, Lady Beatris was the auld MacDonnell laird's wife and distant cousin before marrying ma father. She grew up on those lands and still has kin there."

"That may explain where Alan was trying to take Mairghread, but that doesnae explain where she is now or who took her." Magnus commented.

"We ride to the MacDonnell keep," Tristan decided. "I dinna look forward to telling Beatris that her son is dead, but they may help us search for Mairghread. We keep an eye open for her or anyone who might ken where she was taken."

CHAPTER 11

Mairghread's head pounded like the inside of a church bell. Bile rose in the back of her throat, and she gagged. As her mind cleared, she realized there was a wad of material shoved in her mouth. She cracked her eyes open, but the sunlight made them sting. She looked out from under her eyelashes to check her surroundings. There wasn't much to observe, but what she glimpsed disoriented her. She was in a chamber, but not one she recognized. Mairghread stilled and listened to determine if she was alone. She didn't hear anyone moving around but sensed she wasn't alone. Her heart raced again, making her chest ache after her earlier strain. She felt waterlogged, and her nose burned, making her want to sneeze. Her ears felt like something fuzzing filled them.

"Ye can cease pretending to be asleep. I ken ye're awake now."

Mairghread recognized the voice and wanted to scream and thrash. She realized not only was she gagged, but someone had bound her to the bed. They had tied her wrists and ankles to the bed posts. With her kirtle torn away, she panicked that she was on display for anyone walking by. She breathed once more when the sheet brushed her legs.

Sorcha looked down at her. The sneer of victory on the scorned woman's face told Mairghread all she needed to know. Alan and Sorcha plotted to have her kidnapped, and even though Alan was nowhere in sight, Sorcha was there to make Mairghread even more miserable. "Ye thought ye'd gotten away from Alan. Ye thought ye'd gained yer freedom. The eejit may nae have been able to hold on to ye, but I willna let ye go till I am done with ye."

Mairghread breathed through her nose and tried to calm her rising panic. She no longer feared Alan raping her, but she feared Sorcha's bitterness and vindictiveness much more. Mairghread understood a woman could be far crueler in her jealousy than a man. She tried to piece together what had happened since she pulled herself out of the river. She vaguely remembered two people dragging her along the mud, but she hadn't had the strength to look around. Blackness kept overtaking her every time she tried to open her eyes. She recalled a sense of floating, but now she realized someone must have been carrying her. Mairghread looked again at Sorcha. There was no way she carried Mairghread anywhere, which meant another man had been there to do Sorcha's bidding. Mairghread was noticing the various aches and pains in her body after the fall from the horse, the painful but short ride on Alan's lap, and then the icy swim she took. She also became acutely aware that she was naked under the sheet.

Bluidy bleeding hell! I'm bound, gagged, and naked with nay memory of how I came to be in this position. Ma betrothed's scorned lover is holding me captive after ma scorned whatever Alan was to me lost me in a river. How the bluidy hell am I going to get out of this? I'm certain Tristan is looking for me, but does he even have a clue where I am? I dinna ken where I am. I canna even ask since I've this rag in ma mouth.

Mairghread looked around the chamber as she tried to get her bearings for what seemed like the umpteenth time that day. It was a well-appointed the chamber with glass in the windows and tapestries on the wall to cut down the chill. She noticed clean rushes on the floor. The bed upon which they tied her had a soft mattress and clean sheets with blankets and furs at the foot of the bed. Just as Mairghread calmed since she realized she was in a keep somewhere, her world tilted again.

"Och, the chit is awake?" Mairghread turned her head toward the door as Beatris entered. The older woman moved to Mairghread's bedside and looked down at her. "Ye were so sure ye were too good for ma son, but tis ma son who is too good for ye. We have heard all aboot how ye've been carrying on with Tristan. He's used ye more than a tavern wench in an alley."

Mairghread squinted her eyes as she took in Beatris's pinched face. The longer Mairghread stared at her, the redder her face grew. Before Mairghread changed her expression, Beatris's hand whipped across her cheek, making it sting and smart. Mairghread refused to flinch or allow her eyes to water despite how much her cheek hurt. This only infuriated Beatris more. She slapped Mairghread twice more before Sorcha grabbed her wrist.

"As much as I would like to do the same, marking her face will make her harder to sell."

Sell! What are they talking aboot?

Mairghread looked back and forth between the two women. Beatris looked back down at Mairghread and smirked at her confusion. "Aye, we plan to sell ye to a Norse slaver who comes by every fall. Ye will be a Norseman's bed slave before Christmastide." Beatris cackled as she moved across the room. Before leaving, she turned back to Mairghread. "I hope ye learned something from Tristan's time between yer thighs. Ye'll need that knowledge if ye hope to survive yer new master." Beatris's laugh floated to Mairghread even after the door closed.

"Dinna pretend to be so shocked. Nay woman who holds Tristan's interest is an innocent. He likes his women to ken their way around a cock. If he's still sniffing at yer skirts, ye must do something right to his cock." Sorcha sneered at Mairghread as she, too, moved to the door and then left. Alone, Mairghread tried to process everything she just learned. They assumed her to no longer be a virgin, and they planned to sell her to a Norse slave trader.

How the hell am I going to get out of this? I'm still bound and gagged and naked. Naught aboot that has changed. I have two women ready to send me to ma death or a life of hell, and I still dinna ken where I am. Tristan couldnae ken Sorcha is with Beatris, and even though he kens where he sent Beatris, he canna ken they have me. Where did he say he sent Beatris?

Mairghread's normally steal trap memory failed to recall which clan Tristan said Beatris was from. Her mind was fuzzy from exhaustion and the physical pain she was in. She shifted on the bed, trying to ease the tension in her shoulders, but it only made her moan from the pain that shot through every part of her. Her eyes closed, and she felt herself drifting. She was just about to fall asleep when the door creaked. Her eyes flew open as a young woman of about eighteen or nineteen summers entered the room. Mairghread took in the girl's plaid pattern. *MacDonnells!* At least now she knew where she was. The woman carried a tray with food on it. Mairghread's stomach growled as the scents wafted toward her. She realized she hadn't eaten since breaking her fast earlier that morning. She looked out the window to a setting sun.

"Ma lady, I will remove yer gag but ken there are two guards outside yer door. If ye scream, they will come in." The young woman allowed her eyes to trail over Mairghread's restrained body. With only a thin sheet covering her, it was better than nothing, but left little to the imagination. The maid set the tray down and inched toward the bed. She approached as though she were nearing an injured wild animal. Mairghread tried to relax her body and her expression, so the woman would realize she had nothing to fear. The woman untied the gag from Mairghread's mouth. Her throat ached, and her jaw was sore from being pried open for so long.

"Water," Mairghread whispered. Her voice was rough from whistling as loud as she could and the burning gasps of air she'd taken while in the river.. "Please."

"Here ye are, ma lady." The young maid placed a waterskin to Mairghread's lips and allowed her to drink. "Nae too much too soon, or ye will be ill."

After sipping, Mairghread expected her voice would be closer to normal, so she attempted speaking again. It was still craggy but much stronger. "Who are ye? What's yer name?"

The young woman looked wary to answer but did, anyway. "I'm Alyson."

Alyson. Just like ma Alys back home. Perhaps she will help me.

"Alyson, ye're a MacDonnell, right? Is that where we are? The MacDonnell keep?"

Alyson only nodded her head. She looked toward the door and put a finger to her lips. She neared Mairghread's head and leaned forward to whisper in her ear, "I dinna ken who else might be in the passageway. I am only to feed ye and allow ye to use the chamber pot. They warned me nae to speak to ye, but I dinna think this is right. They shouldnae tie ye up like a boar waiting for the spit."

While Mairghread didn't appreciate the comparison to a grizzly boar, the similarities didn't escape her. She couldn't help but smile. Alyson looked at her as if she had gone soft in the head.

"If I dinna smile, then I will surely start crying. I dinna even ken how I got here, but I ken Beatris and Sorcha plan me harm. If they succeed, they will start a clan war between the MacDonnells, and the Sinclairs and Mackays. Neither ma father nor ma betrothed will stand for this. Once ma family is involved, so will be the Sutherlands, ma mama's people."

"Isnae Alan yer betrothed? I was under the impression he was why ye were here."

"Nay!" Mairghread answered in a harsh whisper. "Alan stole me from Mackay lands, then lost me in the river. I washed up on the shore, and the next thing I kenned I was waking up here to find Sorcha and Beatris planning to sell me to a Norse slaver." Mairghread wasn't sure why she shared all of this with Alyson, but she was overwhelmed and, frankly, terrified.

A knock came on the door, and it opened a crack. A guard stuck his nose in and looked around. When his eyes landed on Mairghread, he leered at her and licked his lips. He looked over at Alyson. "Yer time is up. Come now."

"Nonsense, Duncan. Ye ken I just walked in. I must still feed Lady Mairghread. Close the door and wait for me to come out. Open it again, and I'll tell the laird ye've been harassing his guest."

When the door closed, Mairghread raised her eyebrows. "Guest?"

"Aye. Nay one kens who ye are, and nay one kens ye're tied up and gagged. Lady Beatris and Sorcha didna tell anyone who ye are, and they definitely didna tell the laird what they did or why they placed guards at yer door. I only ken because Sorcha is ma cousin, and she forced me to serve ye. Nay offense intended, ma lady." Alyson's cheeks pinkened when she realized how the last part came out.

"Dinna be embarrassed. I am more than enough embarrassed for both of us. Sorcha is yer cousin? Does that mean she's a MacDonnell?"

"Nay, ma lady. Sorcha and her parents are Mackays. I am, too, but ma mother remarried a MacDonnell when I was still a wean. We moved here, and I have been here ever since."

"How does yer laird nae ken he has a prisoner in one of his guest chambers?"

"Lady Beatris and Sorcha pretended nae to recognize ye. Sorcha and a guardsman brought ye to the keep. They claimed to find ye by the river. Ye were soaking wet, and yer kirtle was in tatters. It was such a distraction that nay body asked why they were there. It seemed to make sense. Lady Beatris had them bring ye abovestairs, and both women promised to tend to ye. The laird agreed as he gives in to Lady Beatris to keep the peace. He canna stand his stepmother."

"Stepmother? How is that? She's Laird Mackay's stepmother too."

Alyson brought a bowl of steaming broth over to the bedside. She put it down on the table next to the bed and moved the pillows behind Mairghread's head and shoulders to prop her up enough so she could swallow without choking. She held the bowl to Mairghread's lips and let her sip.

"Aye well, Lady Beatris married the auld laird after his first wife died. Lady Mary, the auld laird's first wife, had already birthed two sons and three daughters before she passed. Lady Beatris arrived a short time later because the laird needed a mother for his children. She didna take any interest in the bairns and weans once the auld laird wedded and bedded her. Her belly started swelling with Alan within four moons. As I've heard it, it raised some eyebrows. But the auld laird liked his pretty, young bride, though she still left the auld laird's children without a mother. Lady Beatris spoiled Alan when he was a wean, and his aulder brothers and sisters didna take to him. When the current laird became chief, Lady Beatris left to marry Laird Mackay. Alan was about three or four, I believe."

In all her conversations with Tristan, Lady Beatris and Alan's history before arriving at the Mackays never came up. Mairghread wondered how much Tristan knew. "How have Lady Beatris and Sorcha settled in to being here now? What aboot Alan? How long has Sorcha been here?" Mairghread had thought Sorcha was still living in a croft on her own. She hadn't known Sorcha left Mackay land.

"Lady Beatris and Alan arrived with Mackay guards several sennights ago. Sorcha only arrived less than a sennight ago. Lady Beatris claimed Sorcha was her maid from when she lived with the Mackays, and that she needed Sorcha's help, that nay one was better at dressing her hair than Sorcha. Alan seemed keen to have Sorcha keep him company most nights since none of the MacDonnell women want to warm his bed. The laird has already had to stop Alan from assaulting more than one woman in the keep."

"Sorcha wasna Lady Beatris's maid at the Mackay keep. Sorcha was a kitchen servant and server along with the laird's lover." It galled Mairghread to admit that out loud, but there was nothing she could do that would change the past. She couldn't undo Tristan's history with other women, and if she were being honest with herself, she benefited immensely from Tristan's practice before she came along.

"Sorcha was Laird Mackay's lover? She's now Alan's. They seemed to ken each other vera well when she arrived. Vera well indeed."

"I wonder if Alan was bedding her while Tristan was, too. It wouldnae surprise me in the least."

By now, Mairghread had finished the broth and the bit of crusty bread that went with it. Alyson cleaned up and replaced the bowl on the tray. She looked at Mairghread and shook her head.

"Ma lady, I canna untie ye. Lady Beatris or Sorcha would nay doubt kill me if they found ye free. But I also canna bring maself to gag ye either. Will ye promise nae to scream or even make a peep? If ye will remain silent, I willna gag ye."

"I will remain silent." *For now.* "Thank ye for yer kindness."

"Aye, well, I will be back before I retire for the night. I will bring more broth and help ye with the chamber pot if needed."

Mairghread could only nod her head to that. She realized that meant she wasn't even going to be untied to use the necessary if Alyson was offering to assist her with the chamber pot.

How bluidy humiliating. Hmm. I canna even remember how many times I have sworn today. I willna be able to confess all of them. I doubt I'm done for the day, either. If either of those bitches return—well there's one more—I dinna think I can stop maself from heaping more curses upon them.

Mairghread looked out the window again. The sun had set. It was evening, and she barely made out the sounds of people gathering in the Great Hall below. She was overwhelmingly tired.

If I just close ma eyes for a wee while, I will regain ma strength for when I need to fight. For a fight I will give them if they think to give me over to a Norseman.

CHAPTER 12

The search party made up of Mackay warriors, the Mackay laird, and the brothers Sinclair arrived at the MacDonnell keep just as servants laid out the evening meal. Tristan and the Sinclairs entered the Great Hall with a contingent of MacDonnell warriors surrounding them. They had agreed to surrender their weapons before entering the keep, but each of them had at least one dirk hidden in a boot. No warrior was ever without a weapon. Tristan looked around and spotted Lady Beatris seated at the dais. Two chairs down from her was the current laird, Malcolm MacDonnell. Laird MacDonnell looked up as the visitors approached the dais. He looked surprised to see Mackays and Sinclairs entering his keep together. Peacefully.

"To what do I owe this surprise visit?" Malcolm boomed from his seat. He stood and moved down to the floor to greet his guests. "Tristan, I havenae seen ye in ages. How are ye? Since when have ye become friendly with the Sinclairs?" While the McDonnells and Sinclairs lived far enough apart that they couldn't easily antagonize one another, they weren't exactly warm to one another either. The four Sinclair brothers assumed their usual position of a semicircle with their arms crossed and feet planted hip-width apart.

"Malcolm, I'm betrothed to Lady Mairghread Sinclair. Our mutual brother stole her from ma land today. Was she brought here?"

"Alan? Nay. I havenae seen him all day."

"I didna ask if Alan was here. I ken where he is. What I dinna ken is where ma woman is." Tristan growled the last part. Malcolm's eyebrows shot up. He had fair hair, fair skin, and fair eyebrows, so his eyebrows seemed almost to disappear. He turned his sharp blue eyes on his former stepmother, who eyed the group of men warily. As she rose, Malcolm grasped Tristan's arm and waved him toward his solar. "If ye want to learn aught, this is nae the place to do it. Ye ken she will only interfere. Come to ma solar. All of ye."

The men made their way to the back of the Great Hall and entered Laird MacDonnell's private sanctum. A small fire burning in the hearth warmed his solar. There were plenty of chairs available, and a large round table sat in the center. Laird MacDonnell moved to the sideboard and pulled out tin cups and a bottle of whisky. He poured and handed them out. Before speaking again, he took a long draw from his own cup. He looked at the Mackay and each of the Sinclairs. They looked haggard and impatient. He could only imagine what his bastard of a half-brother had done now. "As I said, I havenae seen Alan all day. He rode out early this morning and hasnae returned."

"And I told ye I ken where he is. He's dead and tied to a horse in yer bailey."

"What!" Before Malcom got any further, there was a soft knock. "Enter!"

Alyson entered with a tray overflowing with trenchers. She eased into the room and placed the tray on the table. With her head down, she moved about the table, handing out the trenchers of steaming stew. As she moved next to Magnus, he dipped his head to look at her face.

"Thank ye, lass. Ma stomach thought ma mouth ran away." Alyson giggled and blushed. She looked up and saw Magnus's face for the first time. She gasped and dropped the trencher she was about to place before Magnus. "Lass, are ye all right? What is it? I didna ken I was that ugly."

"Ye're—ye're—ye're. Well, ye're ye." Alyson stammered, unable to gather her thoughts. She was looking at Lady Mairghread's face, but the masculine version. And instead of stormy, angry blue-gray eyes, there were warm, whisky-brown eyes staring at her. Alyson looked around the table and shook. "Ye're her brothers, arenae ye?"

"Where is she?" Tristan bellowed, as he shoved his chair back. He reached across to Malcolm and grabbed his leine. "Where is Mairghread? What the hell have ye done with her?"

Malcolm tried to break Tristan's grip, but Tristan only yanked harder. He only moved Malcolm an inch, as they were well matched in height, size, and strength. "Ye come to ma keep and begin accusing me of what I dinna even ken!"

"Ma lairds, please. I can explain. Please." Alyson looked to Magnus for help. He was the only enormous man in the room who didn't terrify her.

"Tristan, calm down. Ye're scaring the lass too badly for her to talk." Magnus stood and wrapped an arm around Alyson. "Come now, lass what is it ye ken? What can ye tell us? Ye can see Laird Mackay is out of his mind with worry."

Alyson looked up at Magnus and smiled shyly. She turned to examine the other men, who all wore an expectant expression on their faces. "Sorcha brought Lady Mairghread in today."

"Sorcha? What is she doing here?" Tavish piped in. "I thought she was still on Mackay land."

"As did I. Nay one reported to me that she left." Tristan didn't know who to direct his anger at now. Malcolm for having his beloved. Sorcha, for whatever her involvement was. Or his guardsmen who had failed to report Sorcha left her croft and Mackay land altogether.

"Sorcha arrived about a sennight ago and claimed to be our stepmother's maid. Lady Beatris welcomed her as though she kenned her well and said she couldnae live any longer without Sorcha's help," Malcolm explained.

"Sorcha isnae a lady's maid. She's barely a kitchen maid." Tristan looked to Alyson, trying to smile and encourage her. He feared it came out as nothing more than a grimace.

"Aye, well, Sorcha kenned Lady Beatris and Alan vera well. She seemed to ken Alan better than any of the other women here." Alyson couldn't help the blush that overcame her, but she continued to tell the tale. "Today, Sorcha and a guard brought in a woman who looked half drowned. They said they were walking near the river and found her washed up on the shore. Lady Beatris offered to care for the woman, and they took her to a guest chamber. They sent me up with a tray just a short while ago. When I removed the gag from her mouth, the woman told me her name was Lady Mairghread and that they took her from Mackay land."

"Gag? Where is she? Where is she now? I will see her now!" This time there was no doubt Tristan roared. Alyson backed up to the solid wall of Magnus's chest behind her. He placed a hand on her waist to balance her.

"Ye were just told they placed her in one of the guest chambers. She is being well taken care of, I assure ye." Malcolm MacDonnell cut in.

"Nay, she isnae." Alyson only whispered this.

Tristan turned on her and looked ready to murder her. "Where. Is. She?"

"Tristan, come I will take ye to her." Malcolm moved toward the door of the solar. Tristan and the Sinclairs moved as one.

"Alyson, stay out of sight. I dinna want Lady Beatris or

Sorcha to ken ye told us aught." Magnus gave her a smile as he followed the other men out of the room. The group of men had just made it to the landing when a loud crash from an abovestairs chamber echoed through the passageway. Then there was the sound of something breaking and a scream, followed by a loud grunt.

"Mairghread!" Tristan took off at a run toward the noise. The sight that met his eyes would be forever engrained into his mind's eye. He could never unsee it. There on the bed laid the one great love of his life. Mairghread had one arm and both of her legs tied to the bed posts. She was naked, and two men were attempting to defile her. She was swinging her free arm wildly as she landed punch after punch to one man's head, but it seemed not to faze him as he licked her breast. She was bucking her body as she tried to shove both men off her. Another man was leaning between her legs with his tongue hanging out.

"Nay! Nay! Ye canna touch me! I will kill ye both before ye are through." Her worn out voice came out between a scream and a whisper.

Tristan felt the rage boil up and out of him. He was seeing red before, but now, just like in the heat of battle, his vision tunneled to black on the edges and crisp clearness in the center. He launched himself at the bed and tackled the man between her legs. They crashed to the ground, and he straddled the man. His fists flew one after the other as he pummeled the assailant. The other man's head hit the hard floor with a nasty crack, but he still struggled to push Tristan off him. It was only a matter of a minute or two before the man breathed his last. Tristan had beaten him to death with his bare hands. Tristan wasn't even close to being done yet. He jumped from the man and spun around. Alexander and Tavish had the other attacker pinned to the ground. As Tavish held him, Alexander gutted him with his dirk. Callum was untying Mairghread as Magnus pulled the sheet and blankets over her naked body.

Tristan pushed past Callum and scooped Mairghread into his arms. He didn't spare a glance at anyone other than Mairghread as she wrapped her arms around his neck. He walked to the passageway and turned to the chamber next door, unsure where he was going. He was only certain he had to get Mairghread out of the chamber where they kept her prisoner. Tristan looked around and didn't think Mairghread would want him to place her on another bed just yet. He moved to the chair in front of the fire and sat down. He arranged her in his lap and held her. He kissed her forehead over and over as he whispered over and over, "*tha gràdh agam.*"

Mairghread burrowed into his chest as though she were trying to become a part of him. "I love ye, too," was all she managed between sobs. She tried to slow her breathing and to sit up, but she was too weak. "Kiss," she whispered.

Tristan looked down at her watery eyes and couldn't imagine a more wondrous sight than her in his arms at that moment. He brushed his lips against hers. He didn't want to frighten or traumatize her any more than she already was. However, she wasn't content with a light kiss. She pulled on his neck and raised her chin. She licked the seal of his lips and pressed harder with hers. Tristan wouldn't have turned her down, even if he wanted to. The kiss deepened, and his hands roamed over her body. He had a tiny thought in the back of his head that he was checking her for injuries just as much as he was enjoying the feel of her in his arms. They had barely begun when the door slammed open. Mairghread yelped and cowered in his arms. Tristan looked down at her and wasn't happy to find fear there. He looked over his shoulder to discover who had entered.

"Ye canna just carry our sister off and hide her from us," Callum growled.

"Mairghread, are ye all right, lass? Are ye hurt?" Magnus squatted next to the chair Tristan and Mairghread shared. He looked her over and reached out to tuck her hair behind her ears. A brotherly move he'd done countless times over the years. "Come here, lass."

Mairghread could only shake her head and cling tighter to Tristan. She leaned her head against his broad chest and closed her eyes. She breathed in his musky scent. It was the first sense of calm she had experienced since before they rode out of the gates that morning. Tristan tightened his hold on her and glared at Magnus.

Magnus stood up and exchanged looks with his brothers. He looked down at his wee sister, who was now clearly a woman. A woman who had chosen her man over her brothers. If any of them had been willing to speak their feelings, they might have admitted it hurt a bit to know she had replaced them. They no longer felt needed. They each shrugged, defeated, and walked out of the room.

Once they were alone again, Tristan sat Mairghread up and looked into her eyes. The fear was no longer there, but a great sadness was. He wondered just what had happened to her in the hours they were apart. Had a man molested her? His mind wouldn't shake the image of the two men just minutes ago. She laid a hand over his heart and just shook her head.

"Ye and ma brothers got here in time. Other than one of them licking ma breast, they didna have time to do aught worse to me. Nay body did aught worse to me."

Tristan couldn't help but breathe a sigh of relief, but he felt Mairghread stiffen in his arms. He knew why she retreated. "*Mo chridhe*, I would love ye and marry ye regardless of whether aught happened. It wouldnae have been yer doing or yer fault. I breathe easier because I'm relieved ye werenae hurt more than I can see."

"Really?"

"Little flame, ye are mine and always will be. I willna ever give ye up nay matter what. I'm proud of how ye tried to defend yerself, but they were both far larger than ye, and ye were tied down. Even if we hadnae been here in time, I wouldnae have turned ye away once we got here."

Mairghread couldn't understand why that made her feel so relieved, but it did. She realized she worried he might find her dirty or used after what he witnessed. She also realized she should have given Tristan more credit. "I'm just so thankful ye came when ye did. I kenned ye'd find me eventually, but I had nay idea when that might be. I figured it would be days or even sennights before ye tracked me. How did ye ken I was here?"

"We didna. At least, nae when we first arrived. We found the spot where ye climbed out of the water, and someone dragged ye to the top of the embankment. We found three sets of footprints, but then there was naught. Yer brothers and I came hoping whoever rescued ye might have brought ye here. If ye were nae here, we hoped the McDonnells might help us search their lands. When we arrived, we spotted Beatris at the dais. We moved to Malcolm's solar to talk, but before we even got vera far, a young woman brought in food. Her name was Alyson, and she said she kenned ye were here."

"Alyson was kind to me. She unbound ma gag and fed me, and she said she would come back later with more food and to help me if I needed it." Mairghread couldn't bring herself to admit it was to help with the chamber pot. Tristan looked at her and seemed to understand without an explanation. He looked at her wrists, raw from being bound. "She couldnae untie me or else Sorcha and Beatris would ken who did it. Did ye ken Sorcha is here?"

"Aye. I didna before, but I do now. I havenae seen her, which is just as well because I will strangle her. If Alyson didna untie ye, how did one hand become free?"

Mairghread paused before she answered that. She was certain the truth would upset Tristan, but she also wouldn't lie. The truth would need to be told to Laird MacDonnell, as it was his men who meant to rape her. She took a slow breath before answering. "The mon, Donald, who was licking ma breast untied ma hand. He forced me to—"

Mairghread couldn't bring herself to say it after all. Mairghread looked at her hand, suddenly unable to wait to get it clean. She stood up from Tristan's lap and wrapped the sheet and blanket around her. She walked over to the wash basin and scrubbed her hands. Tristan came up behind her and tenderly removed the soap, pressing them into the water. Tristan ran his large, calloused hands over hers as though she were made of the softest silk. He lifted them and wrapped a drying cloth over them before he dried her hands and turned her toward him. He smiled at her and nodded his head. She took another long breath.

"He forced me to stroke him until he was hard." Mairghread tried to swallow her sob and buried her face in his chest. "I'm sorry. I'm so, so sorry."

Tristan stepped back, and Mairghread whimpered, fearing he was rejecting her. He wrapped one arm around her and pulled her to his chest. He used his other hand to lift her chin, but she wouldn't make eye contact. "What on God's green earth do ye have to be sorry for? He forced ye. Ye said it, and I said I saw how much larger he was than ye. I ken ye didna do it willingly. Mairghread, I dinna blame ye for any of this. It wasna yer fault. It was Alan's fault for stealing ye away. It was Beatris and Sorcha's fault for having ye bound and for leaving ye those so-called guards. It was Laird MacDonnell's fault for having guardsmen who assume they can abuse and assault women. And it's mine for nae protecting ye better. I should have listened to ye and brought ye back with me."

Mairghread looked up with watery eyes and stared at him. "How did I get to be so fortunate as to be loved by a mon such as ye?"

"Fortune has naught to do with it. It's because ye are a warm, intelligent, quick witted, strong woman, who is mighty easy to love. I fell in love with ye from the vera start."

Mairghread stepped into Tristan's embrace and wrapped her arms around his waist. Another wave of exhaustion overcame her, and she failed to stifle her yawn, even though she tried. Tristan kissed the top of her head and scooped her into his arms. Once more, he looked at the bed but wasn't sure she was ready for it yet. He returned them to the chair where he sat and stroked her head and back. Her body went limp only moments after they settled. He looked down at this woman who held his heart. He had never suffered the amount of fear that he had on this day. Not even going into battle or becoming laird at a young age had made him so terrified as the threat that he might have lost Mairghread or that someone harmed her.

Neither had such an overpowering amount of rage consumed Tristan as when he learned Mairghread was here, and then when he found her in the chamber next door. The bloodlust and killing rage would have scared him, too, if he hadn't been so intent upon rescuing her and punishing the offenders. As he continued to stroke her hair and back, he realized a series of things in rapid succession. First, he would marry her before the sun set the next day. He didn't care who officiated, who was there, or where it happened. He would call Mairghread "wife" before the next night started. Second, he had to deal with Beatris and Sorcha's parts in all of this. Third, he and Laird MacDonnell would have a reckoning on how his guards behaved.

Once Mairghread twitched twice and her breathing slowed, she convinced him that she was in a deep sleep. He moved her to the bed and laid her down. Tristan didn't want to leave her for even a second, but he was certain he didn't want to deal with this mess while she was present. He wanted to shield her from any more nastiness, and he was certain nastiness was all that was inevitable where it concerned Beatris and Sorcha. He placed a soft kiss on her lips and moved to the door.

What looked like a large boulder lurched backwards when Tristan opened the door. He looked down to discover Magnus sitting in the doorframe. Magnus stood up and turned to Tristan. His eyes were red rimmed and glassy. What Tristan faced shocked him. It was obvious Magnus had been crying, and the mountain of a man didn't seem to care to hide it. Magnus peered around Tristan and spotted Mairghread on the bed.

"Is she well?" Magnus whispered.

"Aye." Tristan looked back over his shoulder at Mairghread's sleeping form and smiled. "She's exhausted and badly shaken, but well. She says naught untoward happened beyond what we witnessed. She felt guilty and scared I wouldnae forgive her. She could've knocked me over with a feather when she apologized. I made sure she understands I dinna blame her for any of this, and I willna set her aside. Just the opposite, Magnus. I will marry yer sister tomorrow, come hell or high water. I willna wait another day to make her ma wife."

Magnus looked at Tristan and the hard set of his jaw. Determination radiated off him, so Magnus nodded.

"I must see aboot Beatris and Sorcha. I also amnae pleased with MacDonnell's men. Will ye stay with her until I return? I dinna want her to awake to being alone."

"Aye, I'll stay, but ye'll have to get in line for dealing with the MacDonnell. There are three Sinclairs ahead of ye. As for Beatris and Sorcha, och well, ye and MacDonnell are welcome to them. We, Sinclairs, dinna want either of them near any of us."

Magnus pushed past Tristan and pulled the chair from near the fire over to the bedside. Tristan watched as Magnus took Mairghread's tiny hand in his massive one. He bowed his head over her hand, and his shoulders shook. Tristan pulled the door closed to give the brother and sister privacy. It still shocked him that Magnus was crying. But he considered if their positions were reversed. Had they both seen what they had, but he wasn't allowed to comfort Mairghread, he most likely would have been a blubbering mess.

Tristan entered a subdued and empty Great Hall. He looked around to see if he could find any of the people he looked for. An old woman sitting at a trestle table pointed toward the door to the MacDonnell's solar. He marched over and didn't bother to knock before opening the door. The scene that met him wasn't what he expected, but he should have known.

Malcolm sat behind his desk with Callum leaning across the table glaring at him and yelling. Sorcha was near the fireplace with crocodile tears falling down her cheeks as she tried to bat her eyelashes at a disgusted and disinterested Tavish. Beatris sat at the table with a furious Alexander standing over her.

"How could ye nae ken who they brought into yer keep? A guest? Who the bluidy hell did ye think she was? Did ye nae look at her at all? She looks just like our father and all of us. Anyone would ken she's a Sinclair with just one peek." Callum's voice rose louder with each word. "Ye useless piece of shite. What type of men do ye have in yer clan who would rape a woman? Is that yer idea of Highland hospitality? To let yer men molest an innocent lass, who yer former stepmother and yer servant tied to the bed?"

Before Malcolm was prepared, Callum gripped his large wooden desk and yanked it up. The desk flew against the wall and landed with a massive crash. Callum lunged and grabbed him around the neck. He lifted the large warrior out of his chair and shook him like a rag doll. Tristan moved forward. He wasn't sure if it was to intercede on Malcolm's behalf or to ensure he got his pound of flesh, but a loud banging at the solar door made him turn.

"Ma laird? Ma laird, are ye all right in there? Let us in!" The pounding continued. Tristan made it to the door just as it opened. He wedged himself into the doorway and blocked the entrance.

"We are sorting through some family business in here. Yer laird will live, but dinna disturb us again, nae matter what ye hear." Tristan slammed the door in the guards' faces and dropped the bar into place.

By now Callum had broken Malcolm's nose and jaw. Both eyes were already showing bruising from the broken nose. Tristan walked over and tapped Callum on the shoulder. Callum was ready to swing at Tristan before he realized who he was. Callum let go of Malcolm and stepped aside. An unspoken agreement passed between them. Malcolm was cupping his nose when he looked up at Tristan. Without a word, Tristan punched Malcolm in the gut, then kneed him in the groin.

"Ye are more than just a might lucky we arrived when we did. If yer men had raped ma betrothed, ye would have an all-out war on yer hands with both the Mackays and the Sinclairs. Ye ken it would nae take much for us to summon our allies, who are many and strong. Far more and far stronger than yers." Tristan punched his fellow laird in the gut again. As Malcolm bent over, Tristan thrust his fist up into the underside of the man's chin. "If the king wouldnae be breathing down ma neck, I would kill ye for this offense. Count yerself lucky yet again that I dinna have the time to deal with an angry monarch when I'm aboot to marry the only woman I have ever and will ever love."

The MacDonnell was wise enough to only nod. He was angry that he was being beaten in his own solar by not one clan, but two. However, he understood it was impossible to defend himself against four angry men, and he didn't want his men to catch sight of him as he was. His pride wouldn't allow it. He also had the sense to accept that, to some degree, he deserved it. He hadn't cared who the bedraggled woman was when they brought her in. He was more than willing to allow her a place to rest and recover, but he wasn't interested beyond that. It shocked him to find his two warriors attempting to rape his guest, and he would deal with that because, unlike what the Mackay and the Sinclairs assumed, he didn't tolerate women in his keep being abused by the men of his clan.

"I understand how ye feel. I would feel the same if I were in yer place. However, ma men dinna abuse women. I dinna allow it in ma keep. I canna explain why those two behaved that way, but I assure ye, I will find out." The effort to say that much left Malcom breathless. He fell back into his chair. He could barely see as his eyes continued to swell, but he caught the expression on Sorcha's face as he said he would investigate his men. The smugness made his gut churn. She had something to do with the incident. Of that, he was sure. The woman had entertained him more than once since her arrival, and she knew how to do things to his cock no other woman had, but she wasn't worth a clan war. He was also aware her attention wasn't undivided. She'd been pleasuring Alan, along with many of the guardsmen. Malcom stood from his chair and walked to the fireplace. Tristan and Callum watched him.

"But I didna do aught wrong. I was only helping her. That's why I brought her to safety. I kenned Laird MacDonnell would allow us to care for her, and I assumed Lady Beatris would tell the laird who she was, but Lady Beatris assumed I would tell him. It was just a miscommunication." Sorcha continued her tears as she reached out to grip Tavish's hand, but he brushed it away and took a step back.

"Sorcha, those are lies, and ye ken it. Ye told me ye didna ken who the lass was. Lady Beatris said the same. If ye both kenned who she was, ye should have said as much when ye and Thomas walked in. Yer lies are only digging ye deeper." Malcolm reached out and grabbed a handful of her hair. He rarely manhandled women, but this one and his former stepmother were about to embroil them in a war. He shook her and leaned over to whisper loudly in her ear. "If ye would like to come out of this without losing yer head, I suggest ye start telling the truth. Now, Sorcha."

Sorcha looked around the room filled with large angry men and one bitter old woman. It forced her to accept for the first time her looks and physical charms wouldn't save her. The best she hoped for was to deflect responsibility and blame from herself.

Sorcha pointed at Beatris and said, "She and Alan plotted to kidnap Lady Mairghread. Alan claimed they needed her dowry for them to move on. He came to visit me at ma croft one night aboot a fortnight ago, speaking of how he missed me and couldnae live any longer with the lies. He wanted us to be together but couldnae make it happen without the monies from her dowry. He claimed his mother was bleeding him dry with her demands." She sneered at Beatris, then pouted to the men. "He told me he would wait in the woods with two of his men until he got Lady Mairghread alone. Once he grabbed her, he would take her to a monastery or priory where they'd wed straight away. Lady Beatris agreed to this because she doesnae want to live here anymore but expects to be kept as she is accustomed to living. She's the one who told Alan to get the stupid chit. But he couldnae even manage that much. I only agreed because Alan loved me and couldnae live without me."

This declaration only received guffaws and outright laughs from all the men. Beatris sat stewing at the table. She attempted to stand, but Alexander's hand on her shoulder forced her back into her seat. One glimpse at his glare kept her from rising again. It didn't keep her silent, however.

"This whore opens her legs to any mon who can get it up. She was with Tristan and Alan for years. She couldnae accept neither of ma sons would make her the lady of a keep or even their official leman. Tis why she bribed one of the Mackay guardsmen, one of the men who rode out with Alan, to push the boulder onto Mairghread. She doesnae ken the limits to her charms. When the Sinclair chit didna die, she agreed to help Alan because she didna want to live in that little shack any longer, and she wanted Mairghread to pay for taking Tristan. Alan didna love her any more than Tristan did. And Alan never intended to take Mairghread to a convent. How do ye think Sorcha kenned to be by the river? She told me of a Norse slave trader who frequents this area in autumn. She's the one who convinced me that once Alan had the dowries and grew tired of tupping Mairghread, we should give Mairghread to the Norseman."

"First of all, I amnae yer son and never was. Second, Alan is dead so he willna be getting any dowries from anyone. Thirdly—"

The wailing cry that came from Beatris interrupted Tristan. He realized no one had told Beatris that Alan was dead. He should have known from how calm she had been until now. "Who killed ma son? Alan! Alan!" She gasped. "Nay. Nae ma Alan!"

"He got himself killed by trying to go after Mairghread in water that was too deep. Had he nae tried to take ma bride for his own gain, he might still be here. Instead, he is awaiting burial because he drowned. He's strapped to a horse outside." Tristan struggled but mustered no remorse for breaking the news to his former stepmother in such a brutal way. He was completely and totally done with both Sorcha's and Beatris's machinations. He hadn't known he shared Sorcha with Alan, but he had to admit it hadn't surprised him. Before Mairghread, he might have experienced jealousy or anger over all the deception and betrayal. Now, he was done with trying to find redeeming qualities to his stepbrother. He was done with all of it. All he wanted was to return to Mairghread's chamber and check on her. He walked to the door, but before leaving, he turned to the MacDonnell.

"Do with either of them as ye want, but if I ever lay eyes on them again, I will kill them on the spot, woman or nae. I willna tolerate anyone threatening ma kin. I am only willing to stay here tonight because Mairghread is in nay shape to travel, or else I wouldnae consider being here another moment." With that, Tristan slammed the door and made his way above stairs.

Tristan approached Mairghread's door quietly and opened it slowly. He saw Mairghread was still sleeping, and Magnus was still holding her hand. His shoulders moved with the deep breathing of sleep. Tristan didn't have the heart, nor did he see a reason to wake Magnus. He walked to the empty side of the bed and took off his boots, then climbed into bed and wrapped his arms around Mairghread. In her sleep, she shuffled and cuddled into his spooning body. He was asleep before he took his next breath.

CHAPTER 13

*M*airghread awoke to a scorching heat coming from her back. She feared she was being suffocated. A heavy weight draped across her middle and pinned her to the mattress. She couldn't figure out where she was or what held her down until she took another breath and smelled Tristan's musky scent. She turned her head to find him sleeping next to her. He was the oven behind her, and it was his arm that held her snuggled against him. She noticed a weight on the hand farther away from Tristan. She looked over to find Magnus's two large hands holding onto her much smaller one. He sagged against the bed, asleep too. She relaxed back into Tristan's embrace and enjoyed being in his arms, even if one of her brothers was there, too.

As Mairghread's eyes drifted closed again, she noticed snores coming from the foot of the bed. She attempted to sit up but was trapped, thanks to Tristan. She tried to lift his arm from her waist, but he synched it tighter. She tried again and pulled her hand free from Magnus to use both to lift Tristan's arm. This only ended up awakening both men as she sat up. She looked at them both, then strained to peer over the end of the bed as it was still mostly dark in the room, and only a smattering of stars still twinkled in the early morning sky. There on the floor in various positions were Mairghread's three other brothers. Tavish and Alexander laid head-to-head near the door as guards, with Callum at the foot of the bed. All three had their swords lying next to them.

Tristan looked at Mairghread's bare back and realized she was still naked. He'd been so exhausted and so relieved to climb into bed next to her, he hadn't even noticed that she was bare. He reached out and traced his finger along her spine. He already planned to marry her that very day, and by that night, he could enjoy this same view any time he wanted. Until then, he would enjoy gazing at her bare flesh. Mairghread sucked in a breath as his rough finger trailed down her skin, making her shiver. She didn't need to glance back to be certain Tristan was watching her. He leaned forward and kissed her shoulder.

Magnus watched them and scowled. It didn't please him in the least to wake up to find his naked sister in bed with a man. "Get yer paw of ma wee sister before I take it off altogether!"

"Magnus, haud yer wheesht before ye wake the others." Mairghread whispered.

"Too late, lass. We're awake already. Ye didna think ye could move around in a room full of warriors, and we wouldnae awaken." Tavish grumbled as he sat up. His eyes landed on Tristan sitting entirely too close to his sister. "Get yer bluidy hands off of her now!"

"Tavish!"

"Aye. Remove yerself from that bed sharpish. Get out of this chamber." Callum was gripping the foot of the bed so tightly the wood creaked.

"Callum! Dinna speak to him that way. Dinna any of ye speak to him that way. Ye ken we're betrothed, and that's as good as married. The kirk is the last detail."

"The most important detail," growled Alexander.

"I agree. The kirk is the most important detail and a detail that we'll take care of today." Tristan didn't budge. He draped his arm around Mairghread's shoulder and looked down at her. "Will ye marry me today? As soon as we get back to the Mackay keep, and we assure yer da ye're well."

"Poor Da will be beside himself since he doesnae ken where any of us are."

"He does. I sent a rider back to the keep yesterday. While ye were in here with Tristan, we were below stairs sorting things out." Callum explained he sent one of the Mackay men back to the keep, saying they found Mairghread at the MacDonnells', and that while she was well, she needed a night of rest before being ready to travel.

"Ma thanks to ye for doing that." Tristan rose from the bed and walked around to meet Callum. He stuck out his hand and waited. Callum looked at his hand, then looked at Tristan, then looked at Mairghread before looking at the outstretched hand again. When Tristan didn't squirm an inch, Callum grasped his forearm, and they shook. "Now ye can all get out so Mairghread can have a bath brought up to her."

Tristan walked to the door, stuck his head out, and whispered to someone in the passageway. When he turned back into the room, the four brothers were in their usual semicircle with arms crossed. Tristan couldn't help but laugh. These four men were an intimidating sight, but after waking up to find them all guarding their wee sister, he was sure there was a soft spot in all of them.

"Did ye practice this as lads, or do ye nae even ken what ye're doing?"

"Whatever are ye going on aboot, mon?" Tavish smirked. The four of them understood what Tristan meant, but had no intention of answering him.

"It all started when they used to have to line up in front of Da when they were in trouble. He would go down the line and yell at them before tanning their hides when each of them refused to confess. Stubborn lot. As they grew aulder, Da started taking them out to the lists for their punishments, but they still lined up for their turns. It has just become a natural position for them after all the time they spent in trouble as lads." Mairghread laughed for the first time since the previous morning. It felt good to laugh, and she couldn't help continuing to laugh as all five men turned toward her. Tristan crossed the room and climbed back onto the bed. He gathered her into his arms and held her.

"Little flame, it's so good to hear yer laugh. I would listen to it every day for the rest of ma life. Ye havenae given me an answer aboot whether ye'll marry me today."

Mairghread placed her hands on Tristan's cheeks and pulled his head toward her. She kissed him with a sizzling passion that had her brothers clearing their throats and coughing. She was content to ignore them all. When they separated to catch their breath, she laughed again. "I think I will marry ye today."

After some further argument, Mairghread put her tiny foot down and said Tristan would remain while she bathed. She compromised and agreed to use the screen to block her from his view. However, as soon as her brothers left, she climbed out of bed and let the sheets drop. She walked over to the screen and moved it back to where it had been. It surprised Tristan that she was walking around in front of him bare as the day she was born. She looked at Tristan with mischief in her eyes. She caught the desire and lust in his emerald orbs as he watched her move toward him. His hands clenched at his sides as he tried to keep himself from touching her. She reached out and unhooked the brooch holding his plaid in place. She put it down on the bed. Next, she unfastened the belt holding his sporran and plaid in place. She caught his plaid as it unraveled from his waist. She laid the belt, sporran, and plaid on the bed next to the brooch.

Tristan still didn't move, but his breathing was labored. He watched with awe as she ran her hands under his leine. The sensation of them on his skin made him shudder. She smiled as she looked up at him. Her own look of lust and desire replaced the mischief. She lifted his leine as high as possible, but he was far too tall for her to take it off him. She raised one eyebrow in question. Tristan whipped the shirt over his head and threw it on the bed. She raised her arms out to the side but did nothing else. She was daring and willing to make some of the first moves, but she needed Tristan to take part, too.

Tristan grasped Mairghread's hips and pulled her flush to him. He bent over to kiss her, and her arms wrapped around his neck. His arms encircled her waist as he lifted her off the floor. Mairghread wrapped her legs around his waist and reveled in the feeling of his cock throbbing between them. She tilted her hips to make it rub against her slit. She moaned just as he groaned, looking at each other. They both remembered their time at the loch and how Mairghread had wrapped her legs around his waist, just as she did now.

Tristan carried Mairghread to the tub and stepped in. He eased them into the warm water. It was marvelous on her battered body, which was still sore from the day before. This time the moan she made was from the warm water against her aching body. Tristan looked down and noticed for the first time that there were faint bruises appearing around her ribs and on her back.

"*Mo ghaol*, they hurt ye yesterday. I can see the bruises on ye now."

"I can feel them, too, but naught is that serious. I was lucky to nae have hurt maself more when I fell from the horse or while I was in the river."

Tristan hadn't pressed Mairghread to tell him what

happened, but he was still curious. He desperately wanted to learn everything that happened in the time they were apart, but he worried about upsetting her if he asked. Mairghread ran her hands over his chest and then gave his heart a kiss.

"Tristan, I was so frightened when an arrow hit Firelight. I couldnae understand what was happening at first. Suddenly, I was falling, then I hit the ground, knocking the wind out of me. I tried to get up and run back to the keep, but I couldnae catch ma breath. Next thing I kenned, some mon was pulling me onto his horse. We rode with two other men as the arrows flew toward us. I fought with the mon who took me, and I stabbed him with ma *sgian dubh*. His horse spooked and wouldnae stop or turn. I couldnae get away from Alan as the horse ran straight toward him. He grabbed me and forced me onto his horse. Once we entered the forest, he pulled me from the horse and kept his hand over ma mouth until I shook it free to say I couldnae move so fast in ma skirts. The other mon with Alan took the horses and headed to the west while we moved to the east. I tried to bite him, but he pulled ma hair so hard I saw stars as he dragged me toward the river. I could hear ye and the others as ye got to the woods. I went limp and dropped from his arm. It gave me just enough time to whistle a warning, but Alan put a dirk to ma neck. He didna need to say aught for me to understand his meaning. I could whistle once more as we approached the river. I ken one of ma brothers responded, and there was another whistle, but that one didna sound like any of ma brothers."

Mairghread paused there in her story to run her hands over Tristan's chest and abdomen. It fascinated her how the muscles rippled under her fingers. Hard muscle knotted his stomach. As her fingers trailed down to the water, his cock bobbed at the surface. She bit her lower lip as she contemplated wrapping her hand around his shaft instead of continuing the story. Tristan pulled her lip free of her teeth and leaned forward to nip it with his teeth. She decided the story would have to wait. She wrapped her hands around his iron rod and began the motion she had already learned he loved. Tristan widened his legs beneath her, and his hand slipped below the water to find her heat. He brushed his knuckles along her seam and felt more than heard her low moan. He slid two fingers between her netherlips to test her.

Even in the tub of warm water, Mairghread's feminine wetness coated Tristan's fingers, signaling she was as ready as he was. He thrust three fingers into her, and her hips jerked forward, searching for more. He stroked her with his fingers and used his thumb to rub her nub. She pressed her lips to his and opened her mouth. When he slid his tongue into her mouth, she sucked with a rhythm that matched their stroking hands. She didn't curb the whimpers and moans coming from her. She rocked her hips faster as she ground her mound against his fingers, all while he pushed his hips up as he drove his cock into her hand. His free hand found one of her breasts and massaged it. He pinched her nipple as her insides clenched around his fingers. She tore her mouth from his, and with her free hand, she pressed her other breast up to him. He gladly took her offering as he suckled hard. She felt herself falling over the edge into her release. She stroked him harder and faster, wanting him to join her in her pleasure. He groaned as his cock pulsed and his seed leaked from him.

Mairghread sagged against Tristan's chest as one arm dropped below the water to wrap around his waist, and the other crept up to wrap around his neck. She brushed kisses against his chest as his hands massaged her shoulders and her back. They moved their way down to her backside, where massaged her buttocks, too. While this normally aroused her, this time it was both arousing and relaxing, as she hadn't realized her bottom was sore from the previous day.

In just more than a whisper, she continued her tale. "Alan got fed up of dragging and pushing me, so he hefted me over his shoulder and carried me through the woods to the water. He had ma arms pinned underneath me, and his dirk pressed to ma ribs. I couldnae believe he could move through the woods so silently. He crept along until we got to the water. He put me down and grabbed ma arm, pulling me in to the shallow part, but ma skirts slowed me down. With only one hand to hold them up, I wasna able to make much progress. He was becoming more and more impatient with me. He yanked too hard one time, and I lost ma balance. I fell forward, and the current caught me."

Tristan lifted the hair from her neck and slipped his hand beneath. His soft touch encouraged Mairghread to continue as emotion threatened to choke her.

" I righted maself, but the raging water was too strong, and eventually, he lost his hold on me. I was swept away. I rolled to ma back and noticed moss growing on the trees. I kenned I was being pushed east by the river. I tried whistling that call, but I dinna ken if it reached anyone. I could barely hear maself. I spotted a large tree limb sticking out into the river. I grabbed onto it as I bashed into it and pulled maself into the vee of two branches. I cut the laces to ma kirtle, but it was too tight once it was wet for me to peel it off. Then I cut away the skirts. I got free just as Alan waded in after me. I swam underwater as far as ma lungs would allow before I surfaced near where I got out. I couldnae find Alan anywhere, and I couldnae hear aught at all other than the water. I got maself out and laid down on the bank."

Mairghread closed her eyes with a sigh but then shook her head. Tristan kissed her forehead as she sighed again.

"I just had to rest for a moment, but then everything faded black. The next thing I kenned, Sorcha had one of ma arms, and a different guardsman had the other. They were dragging me up the embankment. I tried to break free as I couldnae imagine either of them intended me well, but I was too weak to do aught. Sorcha gagged me and bound me with rope. The mon threw me over his saddle, and they rode out. The jostling of being held down on ma stomach along with the ground whizzing by made me so ill I passed out again. After that, I canna remember aught but waking up in the chamber next door. I was still gagged, and by then, someone had stripped me and tied me to the bed. Sorcha and Beatris informed me of their plan to sell me to the Norseman. They said he would make me a bed slave."

Mairghread paused before continuing with her story. She was uncertain how Tristan would react when she told him about the men coming into her chamber. She peeked up at him and saw he was patiently waiting for her to continue. He was aware of what part of her story she'd come to, and he wouldn't press her to tell him. He was making it her choice. She wasn't about to keep secrets from him. Both men were dead for their choices, so the least she could do was explain what led up to it.

"After Alyson left, the two guardsmen, Donald and Duncan, came into the chamber. They said Sorcha told them they were free to enjoy themselves. Apparently, she'd told them I was a tavern wench who washed up after a former lover dumped me there. I kenned they kenned that wasna the truth, but they were glad for the excuse to molest me. One of them, the one with the lighter colored hair, Donald, the one ma brother gutted, untied one of ma hands. The mon ye beat was pulling the covers off me as the first one forced ma hand onto his shaft. He forced me to stroke him until he was hard."

Mairghread shuddered as the memory flashed before eyes. Tristan cooed to her softly until she nodded and could carry on.

"The other mon changed places with him and forced me to take hold of him, too. Once they were both ready enough, they started touching me and stroking themselves. They made the mistake of letting go of ma arm, so before either grabbed ma wrist, I snatched the vase on the bedside table and bashed the closer one on the head. I couldnae hit him hard enough because I couldnae feel ma arms after being tied for so long. He slapped ma arm away, and the vase flew out of ma hand. It crashed against the wall. I screamed as loud as I could and kept trying to hit him. I tried to buck them off and break free, but I just couldnae. They had just gotten into the position ye found them in only moments before ye stormed in. If ye hadnae gotten there when ye did—" She wasn't able finish. They both understood what would have happened.

Tristan reached for the soap and washing cloth. He soaped it up and rubbed it along Mairghread's skin. He washed her arms and back, then ran the cloth over both breasts. He rubbed more soap onto the cloth before washing between her legs and then lower. He sat forward and held her head in his hand as he leaned her back so her hair became wet. He lathered the soap between his palms and massaged her scalp, washing the long length of her hair, then reached for the bucket of cool water sitting beside the tub. He poured the water over Mairghread's head to wash out the soap. He wiped the water from her face and the little soap bubbles from near her ears, his kiss filled with affection, before placing the soap back on the table.

Mairghread took it and the washing cloth and lathered Tristan's chest. Once she had soap covering most of the expanse, she rubbed the cloth over the muscled planes. She lathered along each arm and followed it with the cloth. She waggled her finger to show she wanted him to lean forward. She pressed her breasts against his chest as she soaped and scrubbed his back. He hardened even more. As she reached up to wash his hair, her breasts brushed against his chin. He grabbed them and pressed them together, running his tongue over her nipples and alternating sucking each.

Mairghread continued to wash his hair as he laved her breasts and suckled like a starving babe. She kneeled to reach the top of his head, and the tip of his shaft was like a loadstone to her sheath. The tip rubbed against her slit, and she couldn't ignore how desperately she wanted to feel him inside her. She lowered herself onto him and allowed his tip to enter her. She moaned and was ready to sink down onto him. Mairghread had waited more than long enough.

Tristan was lost in his haze of lust for this woman. He had never craved a woman before Mairghread. He had lusted after his fair share, but he had always controlled his desires and turned away from any woman without a second thought. He couldn't have turned away from Mairghread if his life depended upon it. Tristan felt her hot seam pressing against his tip and started to raise his hips to meet her. It was only at the last minute he realized what they were about to do. He grabbed her hips and lifted her up.

"*Mo ghràidh*, we canna do this. I promised ye and yer da that we would wait till we wed to join."

Mairghread had been lost to her own sensations and stared down at him in confusion. It took a moment for her mind to clear and then focus. She shook her head and moaned. "Havenae we waited long enough? Arenae we close enough to the wedding? We are to be wed in just a few hours. It's our wedding day, so why wait any longer?" She was frustrated beyond belief. She figured it was easy for him to turn her away since this wasn't a new and exciting experience for him, but her body veritably ached for the release only coupling would bring. She was unaccustomed to these driving feelings of lust and desire. She didn't yet know how to control her body or her emotions. She looked down at him and almost burst into tears. She turned around to face his feet, to hide her face, and her anger and disappointment. She leaned forward to wash his legs and feet.

When Mairghread turned to face the other direction, she didn't realize she provided Tristan with a perfect view of her backside and her most sacred of space. As she leaned forward, he grasped her backside and squeezed her cheeks apart, kneading them. She pressed her hips back toward him, enjoying the feel of his large hands on her. He ran his thumb up and down the crease between her cheeks to test her reaction. When she didn't pull away, he tapped the hole with the tip of his thumb. She stilled for only a moment and looked back over her shoulder. She met his eyes as she pushed her hips back farther. The tip of his thumb entered her, and she stilled. She continued to stare at Tristan. He recognized the curiosity and desire in her eyes. He pressed his thumb into her a little more just to test her responsiveness. Mairghread pressed down on his hand and took his thumb into her. Tristan sat forward and wrapped his other hand around her breast. He nipped at her earlobe and then sucked on it. Mairghread's hips rocked of their own volition. Her breath escaped her on a sigh.

Tristan pulled his hand free, and Mairghread whimpered. He lifted her out of the tub and stood her up. He climbed out, too. He snatched a drying cloth off the table and dried Mairghread. Once he finished with her, he dried himself. They stood in silence, and Mairghread wasn't sure what to do. She was confused about whether things had ended abruptly, or if they were moving on to something else. She watched Tristan. When he was dry, he looked at the table next to the tub for the scented oil added to the water. He spotted the vial and pulled out the stopper. He brought it to his nose and sniffed to be sure there was nothing added that would irritate their intimate parts if rubbed in. Satisfied that it was just roses, he guided Mairghread over to the bed.

"There is a way we can join without breaching yer maidenhead. I dinna want to deny either of us any longer the need to join, but I willna dishonor ye or break ma word to leave ye a virgin. If ye dinna like what I'm aboot to do, we will stop right away. Ye need only tell me to stop."

Mairghread understood what Tristan was referring to. She remembered the first time he had tapped her bottom hole when they were at the loch, and she found his exploration in the tub only moments ago to be arousing. She looked up at him and nodded.

Tristan poured a few drops of oil on to his hand and coated his cock in it. Mairghread watched and found her mouth watering. She never imagined she would desire taking any man into her mouth, but she longed to suck Tristan's shaft. She turned away from the temptation and stepped to the side of the bed. She leaned forward and braced her forearms onto the bed. Tristan stepped up behind her, and she felt a cool, slick finger pressing against her entrance. She willed herself to relax as Tristan lifted her left leg onto the bed. She looked over her shoulder and caught the intent look on his face. He was just as eager as she was, but she realized her eagerness stemmed from curiosity while his came from experience.

Mairghread attempted to ignore the twinge of jealousy for all the women who came before her. She no longer wanted to watch, so she turned her head forward. Her mind wandered, and she wondered how many times Tristan had taken Sorcha in such a way. Mairghread was still unaware of who the two other women were with whom he'd had relationships. She hadn't wanted to know before, but now she found she did. She was jealous of a wretched woman and two faceless, nameless ones. Her ardor was cooling. She dropped her head and tried to shake away the images running through her mind.

Tristan's other hand wrapped around Mairghread's hips, and he pressed three fingers into her sheath. His thumb rubbed her pleasure point. Mairghread's thoughts vanished as she felt Tristan's hands upon her. She looked back over her shoulder again, catching a glimpse as he held his shaft in his hand. He bent his knees to enter her, and she almost giggled at how awkward he looked. She realized she was too short. She pushed his hand from her, and his head jerked up. She smiled and licked her lips. The confusion on Tristan's face would have been comical in any other situation. Mairghread climbed onto the bed and drew her legs up and apart. She leaned over and rested her chest against her thighs. She lifted her hips and used her hands to hold her bottom cheeks apart. The scene she presented almost made Tristan spill his seed before even entering her.

"Mair, I willna last long. Dear God above, ye are the most desirable woman I have even seen." Tristan wanted to thrust into her and take her hard, but he accepted he couldn't do that. She was an innocent, and her body was untried. He forced himself to breathe and slow down. "Relax, *mo chridhe*. Let me enter ye. I dinna want to hurt ye, and I ken I am a large mon."

Tristan wrapped one arm around her waist as the other hand guided him to her entrance. Once he pushed the tip into her, he moved his hand down to rub her hidden pearl. His other hand wrapped around her as well, and he used three fingers to enter her sheath. He rocked his hips forward to slide in all the way. Once he was in, he stilled. He waited to see how Mairghread reacted to having him in to the hilt. "Are ye well, *mo ghaol?*"

"Aye. It's unlike aught I have experienced before, but I like it. I feel so full." Mairghread wriggled her hips, and Tristan groaned. The sensation was almost more than he could bare. He wanted to thrust and spill himself, but he didn't want to end this before Mairghread found her release, too. She looked back at Tristan and her brow wrinkled.

"Is—is this it?" Mairghread asked timidly.

Tristan couldn't hold back any longer. Mairghread's innocence drove him wild. He growled and pulled back. He rocked his hips, still mindful to be gentle and not thrust. Mairghread pressed her hips back to meet him. His fingers were firm as he worked to bring her to her climax. Mairghread panted as the mixture of pain and pleasure overwhelmed her. Her moans increased. She bit her bottom lip to silence herself. But they still escaped. Tristan pulled his fingers free and pulled her body upright. He turned her chin toward him and covered her mouth with his. Their kiss was rough and passionate. He swallowed her moans but failed to suppress his own grunts and groans.

Mairghread broke off the kiss to pant, "I'm so vera close. Dinna stop. Please just dinna stop."

Tristan didn't think he could have short of the keep being under attack. He knew his body was creeping closer to the edge. He struggled to hold back his release until Mairghread found hers. He kept rubbing her, and his fingers entered her again. He worked her from the front and the back until her entire body tensed, her muscles squeezing him almost painfully, but he was certain she was climaxing. He couldn't wait any longer. His release was longer and harder than he ever expected. Mairghread's body went limp in his arms, and he eased her forward onto the bed. He pulled out of her as gently as possible and climbed onto the bed next to her. She didn't make a sound and didn't move other than to breathe. She lay there for so long Tristan feared something was wrong. He pulled on her shoulder to make her turn toward him. She didn't want to budge.

"Mair, what is it? Did I hurt ye? Why willna ye look at me?" Tristan was frightened he'd pushed her too far. "Please, tell me what's wrong. I canna help ye if I dinna ken what's wrong."

"Naught is wrong," Mairghread whispered. Tristan raised up onto his elbow and leaned over to peer at her face. Tears streamed down her cheeks. He wanted to grab her and force her to look at him, but he was aware it would help nothing. Instead, he sat up and scooped her into his arms.

"Mairghread, I am so vera sorry. I didna mean to hurt ye. We never have to do that again. I am so, so sorry, *mo ghaol*." Tristan was beside himself with guilt that he had hurt her. He had tried to be gentle, and he assumed she was enjoying it. Had he misunderstood the sounds she made? He thought she made the sounds out of pleasure, but was pain the cause?

"Ye didna hurt me. That isnae why I cry." Mairghread wouldn't explain more than that. She tried to pull away and climb off Tristan's lap. They had to hurry to get ready before her brothers came looking for them.

"Dinna pull away from me. I dinna understand what's wrong, and I canna fix it if I dinna ken."

"I dinna need fixing." Mairghread growled.

"Mayhap ye dinna need fixing, but something between us does."

Mairghread puffed out a breath and looked up at him. The concern on his face was so genuine and so deep she didn't turn him away. She took a deep breath again before beginning. "I havenae ever felt so close, so connected, to anyone in ma life. Our bodies were one, and I enjoyed it more than I dreamed I would. At first, I wasna so sure aboot whether ye taking me like that would be enjoyable for me, too. I wanted the connection it would bring us, but then ma mind wandered." The tears came faster, even though she made no sounds. Her silent crying was almost worse for Tristan than her sobs. He suspected where she was going when she said her mind wandered.

"Tristan, I dinna hold yer past against ye. Honestly. What ye did before ye kenned me is yer own business. Everything we do is so new and special to me, but there is naught new and special to ye. I ken ye've done it all before many times. There is naught left just for me. There is naught aboot making love that every other woman who has been with ye doesnae already ken."

Tristan took Mairghread's face in his hands and kissed her cheeks, her nose, her forehead, her eyelids, and then he brushed his lips against hers. "Mairghread, ye are right, but only partially. Aye, I have done all this before, and I've coupled with other women the way I did with ye. I preferred it." Mairghread ripped her face away from his hands and tried to scramble off his lap. "Nay. Stay and let me finish."

Mairghread shook her head and pushed away from Tristan. He wrapped his arms around her.

"This is nae a conversation I pictured us having right at this moment, but it's a conversation ye started, and I will finish. Now be still." Tristan growled and held Mairghread until she stopped wiggling. She gave up because she was resigned to the fact that she wasn't strong enough to break his hold. She refused to look at him. He would settle for her not fighting him. "I preferred this way of coupling because it decreased the chances of me catching the pox or aught else, and it guaranteed I sired nay bastards. I have never spilled ma seed in a woman's sheath. I willna until I am wed. That means ye will be the only woman with whom I do that. I amnae saying I havenae tupped a woman in the traditional way, but I have never made love to a single woman before. I did that for the first time just now. Every time in the past was only about a physical want. It was about finding a release and physical pleasure. There was never, ever any genuine emotion invested in it. That's why I've never had an official mistress. I've never met a woman before ye who I wanted any commitment with. I canna change what I did before ye, and ma experiences have benefited ye in that I ken what I'm doing. But what I just shared with ye is something I havenae shared with anyone else. I have never loved another woman, and I have never poured ma heart into lovemaking. So ye are wrong to assume there's naught new or special between us. It is all new, and all vera special."

Mairghread listened to every word Tristan said. While some parts made her want to crumple up inside, she understood what he was explaining. She looked at him and saw the truth and honesty in his eyes. She laid her head against his chest and closed her eyes, breathing in his unique scent, even though they had just bathed. She turned her face toward him and kissed his chest over his heart. She couldn't bring herself to move from that position.

"Tristan, I love ye so vera much. Each time I am with ye, it is even more intense than aught else I have ever experienced. These feelings along with everything that's happened in the past day are overwhelming. They were too much for me for a moment, but I dinna regret what we just did. It scared me to think I felt more than ye did. That I feel more than ye ever will."

"I love ye with all that I am. I have experienced naught like this before, and all of it is just between the two of us." Tristan kissed the top of Mairghread's head and run his hand up and down her back. He understood her reaction. He would be a jealous beast if the situation were reversed. If there had been any men who had touched her before him, he would have been driven to kill them.

CHAPTER 14

Tristan and Mairghread dressed and gathered their few belongings. A maid brought a kirtle for Mairghread to wear when she came with a tray from which they broke their fast. It was a sure hint her brothers were becoming impatient with her if they sent food. Her brothers wouldn't wait any longer once Tristan and Mairghread arrived below stairs. They were in the Great Hall in less than ten minutes from when the maid brought everything to them.

Callum, Alexander, and Tavish glared at Tristan, and Magnus just smirked at Mairghread. She shrugged and smiled innocently. Her oldest three brothers looked ready to murder Tristan, but she wrapped her arm around his and led him outside. Malcolm waited for them in the bailey. Beatris and Sorcha were thankfully nowhere to be seen. Malcom's face looked the worse for wear. His eyes were blackened, his nose swollen and crooked. He had a large bruise on his jaw. Mairghread looked at him and then each of the five towering men who surrounded her.

"Dinna glare at me. I was with ye the entire time," Magnus whispered to her.

"Laird MacDonnell, thank ye for taking me in and providing me with a gown in which to travel." Mairghread tried to be gracious, but her comment was met with quiet grumbles. She looked around and saw none of the men were as thankful or forgiving as she was. She decided it was best to leave it at that and said no more.

"MacDonnell, thank ye." That was the most Tristan would say to his neighbor. He accepted Malcolm wasn't solely responsible for what happened on his land or in his keep, but his lack of awareness had nearly cost Mairghread her innocence and her life. He wasn't ready to let that go. Malcolm nodded and bid them goodbye. Mairghread noticed there were only five horses left without riders. One wasn't available for her, so she turned to Tristan and followed him. She felt hands wrap around her waist from behind, making her squeal. Magnus carried her toward his horse and was ready to lift her onto the horse's bare back when she kicked him in the shin.

"Put me down, ye wee beastie!" It was laughable, but it was a term Mairghread had used since they were close in size many moons ago. It had stuck, much like the horse named Tavish. She slapped at Magnus's hands and pried his fingers off her. "I amnae riding with ye, and ye ken it."

"Dinna ye think ye spent enough time with yer future groom this morning? The sun is almost overhead, and half the day is gone," Magnus grumbled.

The sun was barely over the horizon, despite how long they spent alone in her chamber. Mairghread pointed to the sky and shook her head. She twisted loose from his grasp and marched over to Tristan's horse, pushing him out of the way, and put her foot in the stirrup. She hoisted herself up and settled into the front of the saddle. She removed her foot from the stirrup and leaned forward. Mairghread looked expectantly at Tristan. He laughed and mounted behind her. He reined his horse around before anyone dared naysay him, and they rode out.

It took the large group several hours to cover the land between the MacDonnell keep and the Mackay keep as they avoided the forest. Mairghread became sleepy and leaned back against Tristan. It was a warm day for early fall, but there was a slight nip to the air.

"Swing yer leg over and rest against me, *mo chridhe*." Tristan found he enjoyed using different terms of endearment and finding more than one way to let Mairghread know she was his heart. Mairghread adjusted her position, and he unpinned the top part of his plaid. He wrapped it around her, just as he had that morning on the battlements when he asked her to stay and consider marrying him. She wrapped her arms around his waist and nestled into his shoulder.

"This is the happiest place on earth for me." Mairghread sighed and closed her eyes.

"On the back of ma horse in the middle of nowhere?" Tristan teased.

Without opening her eyes, Mairghread responded, "In yer arms is the best place to be."

Tristan kissed the top of her head and wrapped his arms around her. If this was the happiest place on earth for her, he wasn't about to deny her.

The Mackays and Sinclairs continued riding for a couple more hours, only stopping to rest and water the horses. Mairghread was deeply asleep and didn't seem to notice when Tristan handed her to Alexander while he dismounted. Tavish took Tristan's horse along with his own, and Tristan found a shady spot to sit with Mairghread cradled in his lap until it was time to mount up again. Tristan had never experienced such contentment as holding Mairghread in his arms.

As desperately as he wanted to marry her, he almost wished the keep was farther away, so he could hold her a little longer. This fierce woman, who could defend herself in many ways, seemed so tiny and vulnerable when he held her. In some ways, it was difficult to reconcile the two images, but he realized it was her trust in him that allowed herself to let go and fall so deeply asleep in his arms, to be vulnerable before him. Tristan swore to himself, in that moment, to never take her for granted and to always protect her. He had failed her miserably, and it had nearly cost them everything. He would never let that happen again. He wouldn't make the same mistake twice.

As they crested the hill in front of the Mackay keep, the bells rang when the guards spotted them. Mairghread stirred and opened her sleepy eyes. She looked up at Tristan and smiled. The sight that met his eyes mesmerized him. She was the most incredible mix of sensuality and innocence. He prayed she never lost all the innocence and that this would be what he awakened to every morning. He leaned forward and kissed her. It was a lingering kiss and would have continued if Callum hadn't spoken up.

"Da is coming and looks fit to be tied."

It was like Callum threw a bucket of cold water on them both. Mairghread sat up so fast she banged her forehead on Tristan's chin. She spun around to find her father galloping toward them, with Alasdair not far behind. They met each other halfway and reined in. Liam jumped from his horse and ran to Tristan's. He pulled Mairghread from Tristan's arms before she even reached for him. He wrapped his arms around her and squeezed. Mairghread noticed her father was shaking as she tried to pull her arms loose to hug him.

"Da! Da, I canna breathe, and I canna hug ye."

Liam loosened his hold only enough for her to wrap her arms around his waist. She still felt him shaking, and something moist dripped onto her nose. For the first time in her life, she watched tears rolling down her father's cheeks. His shoulders shook from the sobs that racked his body.

"Mo nighean leanabh, mo nighean leanabh." Liam wouldn't stop repeating himself as he held her. She was still his baby girl no matter that she was a woman fully grown and to be married soon.

"Da, I am well. Nay actual harm came to me. Ma brothers and Tristan saved me, and I am here." Mairghread breathed in her father's scent and reveled in the safety of his arms. She realized in that moment how much she would miss this when Castle Varrich became her home. She would no longer seek shelter in her father's arms. No matter how comfortable and safe she was with Tristan, nothing would ever replace how being held by her father felt. It was a distinct sensation.

Tristan walked up behind them. He put his hand on Mairghread's back and leaned in to murmur in her ear, "We will visit yer family as often as ye wish." He continued walking over to Alasdair to give and get a report on what transpired while he was away.

Liam listened to his future son-by-marriage's promise, and he loosened his hold. It had worried him that he had run out of time with his daughter, but Tristan's reassurance made him breathe more easily. Liam wiped his face and looked over Mairghread's shoulders to his sons. He held out his arms to all of them. He had been a loving father their entire lives, but affection in the way of embraces for his sons had ended many years ago. However, they didn't hesitate to walk into his outstretched arms. The six Sinclairs hugged for a long time in relief for their safety and to mark the end of an era. By nightfall, Mairghread would be a Mackay.

***

They returned to the keep, and each person had a specific task set before them. Mairghread headed straight to the kitchens to inform Annag that there would be a wedding that afternoon and feast that evening. She reassured Annag everyone would enjoy anything she might prepare in time, and that she must enlist the help of every available woman as the Great Hall would be full. Once she had done that, she made her way to her chamber to air out her wedding gown. She had bathed that morning, and she shivered as she remembered what happened in and out of the tub, but dirt from the road covered her, and she smelled of horse. She would need to bathe again, so she asked Morag to have the tub and hot water sent to her.

Tristan, meanwhile, set off to track down the priest. He found Father Peter in the sanctuary. It seemed to come as little surprise to Father Peter that Tristan wanted the ceremony that afternoon. In fact, Father Peter began preparing for the special Mass the moment the bells peeled.

Liam and Callum collected the purses with Mairghread's dowry and the deeds for her dower land. Tavish, Alexander, and Magnus volunteered to see the brewer and vintner to make sure enough barrels and casks of ale, wine, and whisky would be available. They made sure to sample each for quality control. All of them wobbled a little by the time the men made their way to the loch for baths. Tristan looked around at his soon-to-be extended family. His mother had died before he could remember her. His father had died when he was only a lad of five-and-ten. He had become laird and forced to grow up. He had already been a trained warrior and been to battle, but the weight of being laird wasn't something possible to prepare for until life thrusted it upon him.

Alan and Beatris had been next to no help at all. Beatris had done the bare minimum to keep Castle Varrich running and took little interest in household matters. While Alan turned out to be a fine and strong warrior, he was a disappointment as tánaiste and as Tristan's second. They had assumed Alan would fill those positions once he was old enough and trained for it; however, it never came to be. Tristan could never rely upon him enough, and so with the approval of the council of elders, he named his lifelong friend, Alasdair, as his tánaiste and second as soon as Alan left. Tristan hadn't considered himself lonely because clansmen always surrounded him, and he was never without a willing woman to keep him company, but he realized it was all very superficial. As he watched Liam and his four sons laugh with one another, he longed for the same sense of family and comradery.

"Are ye going to just stand there like a stone or come in and bathe? I dinna suppose ma sister will want to bed a horse or a mon who smells like one," Magnus called from the waterline.

"Watch yer mouth, son. I dinna want to hear aboot ma wee lass doing such things." Liam grumbled halfheartedly. He smiled up at Tristan and waved him forward.

Tristan moved toward the group of men and began removing his clothes. Once he had stripped down, he reached for his bar of soap. He caught the sound of the crunch of loose stones, but before he glanced up, a large Sinclair man grabbed each of his arms and legs. They picked him up and carried him to the rocks and climbed up. They hoisted him high in the air and counted to three. It happened so quickly Tristan was soaring through the air and landing with a splash before he could hold his breath. He emerged and pushed back his hair. There were the five Sinclair men, all naked and laughing at him. They slapped each other on the back and dove in, including Liam, who turned out to be an agile and graceful swimmer despite his age.

"Welcome to the family, brother." Alexander grinned at him.

"Brother!" The other three cheered.

"Son!" Liam bellowed.

Tristan had never felt so welcomed in all his life. He finally had a family again.

Mairghread welcomed the quiet of being able to ready herself alone. She was glad there was no gaggle of women fussing over her hair and tugging on her as she dressed. The only person she missed was her mother. She still remembered her mother, even if the memories had dimmed a little. She remembered her mother had always smelled of violets, but it was her mother who taught her to make lavender and heather oils and soaps. That was why she preferred that scent for herself. Her mother had been loving, and Mairghread had followed her mother around any time she wasn't trailing after her brothers. She remembered how her mother and father used to gaze at one another even after five children. She prayed she and Tristan would be the same as her parents, even as the years passed. She kneeled beside her bed and clasped her hands together in prayer, offering thanksgiving for her family and for Tristan. She then prayed for guidance and strength. Just as she said "amen," a light knock came at her door.

"Come." Mairghread looked up to find her father peeking around the door. When he spied her kneeling, he came to help her up.

"Are ye ready, *mo nighean leanabh?*"

"Aye, Da." Mairghread leaned over and kissed Liam's cheek. "Will I still be yer baby girl once I am married and have bairns of ma own?"

"Of course, lass. Ye are ma only daughter, and ma youngest child. Ye will never outgrow being *mo nighean leanabh*. Dinna tell ye brothers, but I still consider them as *mo ghillean beaga*."

"Da, nae one of them has been a wee lad in almost a score of years. From what Mama used to say, they all came out big enough to join ye in the lists." Liam's eyes grew misty, and he paused as he envisioned his wife, who had long since passed. Mairghread regretted referring to her mother. She put her hand on his arm and squeezed. "Da?"

"*Leannan*, ye remind me more and more of yer mother every

day. Ye may resemble me, but yer eyes and yer spirit have her spark. She was the one great love of ma life and when she died, I feared I wouldnae be able to carry on without her. She left me with the five greatest treasures I have ever beheld. Every day, ye become more like her, and so I ken she never left me, us. I love ye, *leannan*."

Her father had called Mairghread his wee baby girl and sweetheart. Tristan often called her his darling, his heart, and his treasure. The terms of affection made her heart warm as she realized just how well loved she was. Even her brothers teasing her about being so much smaller than them made her realize they loved her and loved protecting her. Her heart felt like it was overflowing.

"Da, I'm ready to get married, but I will never be ready to stop being yer little lass. I love ye too, Da." Mairghread reached up and kissed Liam's cheek again. She took his hand, and he led her to the door.

CHAPTER 15

Tristan waited outside the doors of the kirk with the four Sinclair brothers standing across from him and Alasdair beside him. The entire clan turned out to witness the long-awaited wedding between their laird and the Sinclair lass. Tristan was becoming impatient as he craned his neck to peer over the crowd. He started to worry something was wrong, or that Mairghread changed her mind. Just as he turned and stepped forward to go investigate, "oohs" and "ahs" coming from the back of the crowd reached him. A murmur ran through the crowd as everyone turned to the back. Tristan tried to catch a glimpse, but there were still far too many people in front of him. He heard the brothers snicker and glared at them. Movement caught their eye and as a one, the four giant brothers stilled. Their eyes all widened, and they nudged one another. Tristan spun around and caught his first glimpse of Mairghread.

The crowd had parted to let Mairghread and her father through. Tristan understood the reaction her brothers had when they spotted her. She was radiant in a blue, shimmering kirtle. She had braided the sides of her hair and joined them at the back. The rest of her hair was down, just as he liked it. His feet wouldn't remain where they were. He walked down the steps and into the crowd to meet Mairghread in the middle. He barely spared a glance to Liam. He held out his arm for Mairghread, and she grasped it.

Tristan and Liam accompanied Mairghread to the foot of the steps outside the kirk. Liam placed a soft kiss on her cheek. It would be the last one he gave her before she became another man's wife. He looked up at Tristan, who only had eyes for Mairghread, and he knew in his heart that he had made the right decision in giving his blessing. He was no fool and was aware they would have run off to marry if he hadn't given it. He was glad to be a witness to this occasion.

Mairghread stared at Tristan. She noticed he had bathed because his hair was still damp. He wore a crisp, saffron leine denoting his position as laird. His *breacan feile* was freshly brushed, and his laird's brooch shone. She had never seen a more handsome man. They joined hands as they stood before the priest and spoke their vows. If asked later exactly what they had said, neither would remember. Instead, they would recall the love they shared and promises to be true to one another for the rest of their lives. Once they spoke their vows, the family moved inside the kirk for the wedding Mass.

Tristan was impatient for the Mass to conclude. He rarely minded attending church and often enjoyed the ritual, but today was a different matter. He wanted done with the service and to have Mairghread officially pronounced his wife. He wanted to skip the feast that awaited them and abscond with her to their chamber. He peeked at Mairghread from the corner of his eye and saw she was looking just as frustrated as he felt. Mairghread turned her head and smiled at him. She edged her hand closer to his on the rail and nudged her pinky against his, wrapping it around his finger. They finished the service with their fingers joined. It was the most they dared to do, but the small touch seemed to calm them both, even if only a little.

Father Peter said the last "amen" and announced to the family and a few special guests within the kirk that Tristan and Mairghread were wed. They stood, and Tristan wrapped his hand around Mairghread's waist. Before he had the chance to pull her to him, she stepped into his embrace. Their lips collided in a kiss that was in no way appropriate for a church. Father Peter cleared his throat several times, Liam tsked, and the brothers Sinclair guffawed. But nothing would break the kiss before Tristan and Mairghread were ready. When they pulled apart, Mairghread pressed her fingertips to her lips and looked up at Tristan.

"Wife," Tristan whispered.

"Husband," Mairghread replied.

Tristin scooped Mairghread into his arms and carried her to the kirk's entrance, where he paused for the cheering crowd. He continued to the Great Hall despite her pleas to be put down. When they got halfway across the bailey, Mairghread gave up and laid her head against his shoulder.

"Precisely where ye belong," Tristan breathed next to her ear, and Mairghread sighed.

They entered the Great Hall, which had been beautifully, if not quickly, decorated for the feast. Tristan climbed the dais stairs and sat down in his seat with Mairghread in his lap. She tried to climb out as the hall filled.

"And just where do ye think ye're going, wife?"

"I canna sit in yer lap during the meal. Surely, ye'll let me go now that everyone is arriving. It's unseemly."

"Since when do ye care about propriety? I bet I will find ye covered with dirks when I undress ye."

Mairghread's cheeks flamed with his bold announcement that he would undress her soon. Contemplating about just how soon made her squirm. "One."

"One what?"

"One dirk is all I have on me." Mairghread squirmed again as the idea of Tristan searching under her kirtle for her knife made her body ache.

"If ye dinna stop wriggling on top of ma cock, ye willna be staying here long enough for the first toast."

Mairghread had noticed his hard length pressing against her hip, and it was making her even more restless. She muttered, "What if I dinna want to stay here long enough to listen to the first toast?"

Tristan growled and cupped her chin, pulling her in for a fierce kiss that had a new level of possessiveness she hadn't felt before. She sank into his embrace and returned his kiss with equal ardor and fervor.

"One," Tristan whispered.

"One what?" Tt was Mairghread's turn to answer.

"One course is all we are staying for. Eat enough to tie ye over because I intend to make ye work up an appetite by morning."

Mairghread looked around and saw her family seated at the high table, and the serving women were bringing around trays of food. When a woman placed a trencher in front of them, Mairghread reached forward and filled it. She put a bit of everything within her reach onto it. She felt more than heard Tristan laugh behind her. She speared a piece of venison and cupped her hand below it to keep it from dribbling on her gown. She turned and fed the piece to Tristan. He reached around her and picked up a piece of venison, too. He held it over the trencher and waited for her to lean forward. When his fingertips meet her lips, she licked them and sucked his finger into her mouth. His cock twitched and strained behind his plaid. Mairghread didn't attempt to contain her giggle. She picked up a piece of quail with her fingers and looked over her shoulder as she brought it to her mouth. She paused to be sure Tristan watched. She stuck the tip of her tongue out to catch the sauce before it dripped, before sucking the piece of poultry into her mouth, then licked her fingertips.

Tristan was ready to burst. He'd endured all the teasing he could manage, and they had only just had a couple of bites. He pushed back his chair and stood up. Mairghread squeaked at the sudden change in position. Tristan looked around and nodded his head once before moving to the dais steps. The crowd looked on in shock and confusion, since the meal had just begun. Not everyone had even started eating yet. Tristan charged straight for the stairs and took them by twos. By the time everyone realized the laird and lady were retiring for the evening, there wasn't enough time to make any bawdy comments. Benches pushed back as clan members rushed to follow them upstairs. They wouldn't be shortchanged their viewing of the bedding ceremony.

Tristan used his elbow to push down the handle of his chamber door, then kicked it shut. He strode to the bed and unceremoniously dumped Mairghread onto it. He sprinted back to the door, turned the key in the lock, and dropped the bar into the brackets. Mairghread was about to complain about his treatment when she heard the footsteps in the passageway, then the pounding on the door. She understood why he'd hurried back to the door. She didn't want any witnesses to her first proper bedding.

Tristan hurried back to the bed and helped Mairghread to stand. He put his hands on her shoulders and leaned his forehead against hers, inhaling the fragrance he would always consider hers. He trailed kisses across her forehead to her temple, down her cheek, and to the sensitive flesh behind her ear. He nibbled and sucked when he got to the place where her neck met her shoulder. "They will give up and go away soon enough. I willna share this time with anyone but ye. Ye are mine and mine alone. I willna have any other mon see ye as only I do. I willna have any other mon see yer face when ye find yer release. That is ma privilege and mine alone."

"I willna share ye either. What is the past will remain there. Nay other woman will see what is now mine and mine alone. I dinna want any other woman to see and dream of what ye do to ma body. That is ma privilege and mine alone."

"*Tha mo chridhe a 'faireachdainn dìreach dhut.*" My heart beats only for you.

"*Tha mo anam a 'bruidhinn dìreach riut fhèin.*" My soul speaks only to you.

Tristan and Mairghread undressed each other. In their own minds, they imagined they would feel more rushed to undress, but they savored this time together. They would only ever have one first time, and they both wanted it to last after having waited for what seemed like an eternity. Once Mairghread was bare, Tristan ran his hands over her entire body and down her arms and thighs. He had seen nothing as beautiful as the woman before him, and now he knew he was bound to her forever.

"There isnae a sight dearer to me than ye in this moment. I havenae wanted aught more in ma life than to have ye as ma wife and to make love to ye."

"Tristan, I am yers forever more." Mairghread ran her hungry eyes over him. She still marveled at his raw strength and power. His body was so different from hers, yet they fit each other so well. "Make me yers in every way. Make me yer wife in truth."

Mairghread sat back on the bed and inched toward the pillows. Tristan climbed onto the bed and moved over her. She laid back and reached for him. He braced himself on his elbows and wrapped his arms around her. They pressed their bodies together and held each other for a moment, reveling in the pleasure of being chest to chest, stomach to stomach, hips to hips, and legs to legs. Their kiss was languid as their tongues explored each other's mouth like it was the first time. Mairghread ran her fingers through his hair, and one of Tristan's hand ran along her ribs and down to her thigh. As their hands explored one another, their breathing increased. Mairghread pressed her hips up against his rod. She was convinced it was harder and longer than ever before. She peeked down between them and had a moment of panic that he wouldn't fit.

"Shh, *mo chridhe*. We will fit."

Mairghread looked into Tristan's eyes and knew he meant it. She opened her legs and let her knees fall to the sides. He brought his hand to her mound and brushed his fingers along her seam. He marveled at how wet she was; she was dripping. He inched his way down, but she squeezed his shoulders. He looked up.

"Later. I canna wait any longer to have ye inside me. I dinna need aught else but that. Tristan, ma body aches for ye. It's painful how badly I want ye. Please, dinna make me wait any longer."

Mairghread's words sank in, and Tristan's cock leaked as he looked at her pink netherlips. He wanted to taste her honey, but he would wait for that pleasure. His cock twitched as the tip touched her damp folds. It seemed to have a mind of its own. He looked into Mairghread's eyes as he inched into her. She brought her knees up to widen her entrance. She seemed to sense what to do.

Tristan wrapped one of Mairghread's legs over his hip and slid into her until he brushed against her maidenhead. He was aware it would hurt, and he accepted it was inevitable. But he balked at the idea of bringing her pain. He could see the livid bruises that covered her body. He'd been able to ignore them before, but now he experienced guilt that he would cause her more discomfort. She seemed to read his mind because she wrapped her other leg around his hip and joined her ankles. She ran her hands down his back and gripped his buttocks.

"I'm fine. Or at least I will be once ye stop waiting." With that, Mairghread thrust her hips up and pushed as hard as she could with her hands and heels. She was so wet it took little effort for Tristan to slide all the way in and break her barrier. She tensed and stiffened. Tristan didn't miss her gasp as her body responded to his invasion. His cock wanted nothing more than to thrust and thrust, but his head and heart told him to withdraw. He started to pull out.

"Dinna ye dare leave me like this. Ye have made ma body ache with desire and then ache with a fullness I wasna prepared for. Now ye will fix it by making love to me." Mairghread forced her body to relax, and Tristan held himself still. It was the single hardest physical feat he had ever accomplished, but he wasn't willing to move until she was ready.

Sweat beaded on Tristan's forehead, and his chest ached as he tried to draw in enough air. His arms were shaking a little. Mairghread ran her hand over his forehead and wiped the sweat on the sheet beside her. Then her hands ran up and down his chest. She raised her chin for a kiss just as she raised her hips. Tristan sank his hips into her as his mouth devoured hers. She put her hands back into the grooves along his hips she loved so much. They were the right size for her hands. They moved together. Mairghread didn't stifle her moans and gasps of pleasure. The more noise she made, the wilder Tristan grew. He grunted as he thrust into her. He was being too rough, and he knew it. He tried to slow down, but she shook her head wildly.

"More. More," Mairghread panted over and over.

Tristan was on the verge of losing control. He had never felt like this before. Mairghread was a constant source of firsts for him, and it continuously shocked him since he had considered himself experienced. He could no longer stop the hard surges of his cock as it pounded into her. "Ye feel so good, Mair. I canna stop. I am so close. God, I want ye so much. I canna stop. I canna stop." Each phrase forced between thrusts.

"Dinna stop. More, Tristan. Harder," Mairghread pleaded. "Please, just dinna stop. I'm so close too."

Mairghread arched her back and hips off the bed and erupted. Her sheath clung to Tristan's rod and squeezed every drop from him. Their release was simultaneous and almost violent in its explosion. It seemed to carry on without an end in sight. His release into her arse had convinced him that it was the most intense climax of his life, but it was nothing remotely close to this one.

They clung to one another, Tristan's arms wrapping around her back and his head buried in her neck. Mairghread's arms and legs encircled him like she was climbing a tree. Neither had any desire to loosen their hold or pull away. Several minutes passed while they stayed like this. It was unfathomable to Tristan how he was still hard inside of her. He didn't think there was a single drop of seed left. Mairghread's hands ran up and down his back, and he kissed her neck over and over. She wasn't sure how she felt after all of that, so she shifted her hips side to side. They moaned together. Tristan looked up. He had never moaned in bed before in his life. At least not without a life-threatening injury.

"Lass?"

"Aye, I'm well. I just dinna ken what to say." Mairghread shifted her hips again, and it aroused her all over again. She rubbed her mound against Tristan's pelvis and was ready for a second round. She peeked up at him and noted the confusion on his face. She paused, worried. "Did I do aught wrong?"

"Nay. Just the opposite. Keep moving like that because it's wonderful. I just dinna ken how I can still be hard after spilling what was surely every drop of seed I have. I can feel maself growing again. Ready for more."

Tristan rolled over and brought Mairghread on top of him.

She leaned back to gaze down. He was the most shockingly handsome man that she had ever met, and he was buried deep within her. She had never in her life imagined lovemaking would be so powerful and all consuming. Mairghread assumed making love would exhaust her after what they had just done, but she was ready for another round, too. She rocked her hips as she tested the new position. She didn't understand how it was possible, but he was even deeper than he had been when she was on the bottom.

"I ken ye will be sore after what we just did, so ye can set the pace now."

A jab of dark jealousy tried to take hold as Mairghread knew Tristan spoke from experience. Instead, she leaned forward and kissed him. She circled her hips and rocked. Mairghread knew he liked the sensation because he nibbled her lower lip and dug his fingers into her backside. She increased her pace and tried raising her hips to slide up and down his shaft. She didn't enjoy that as much as rocking and grinding her mound on him. He did nothing to change her pace or rhythm. He thrust up to meet her and continued until she moved in a frenzy.

"So close, Tristan. I'm so close." Tristan reveled in her growing knowledge of her body and what his body did to bring her pleasure. "Tristan!"

Tristan felt her inner muscles clench around his cock, and he thrust as hard as he could into her, finding his own release. "Mairghread!"

Mairghread sank down to Tristan's chest. It was his turn to run his hands up and down her back.

"I didna ken."

"Tristan, what didna ye ken?"

"I had nay idea this is what true lovemaking feels like. It far surpasses aught I have ever done before." Mairghread lifted her head to gaze at him and watched his eyes roll back in his head before he closed his eyes. His whole body went lax.

"Tristan? Tristan?"

"Lass, I amnae dead, but I could die now for I am surely in heaven." Tristan pulled her back down to lie against his chest. It wasn't long before they both fell asleep with him still joined to her.

EPILOGUE

Nine months later

"Alasdair, I dinna give a rat's arse where Beatris is. I dinna care that she is at court and took Sorcha. Let her be the king's problem. He deserves it for being such a pain ma arse. Mind ye, I still amnae pleased I never received a report from the guardsmen I placed at Sorcha's croft. They never alerted me when she left in the middle of the night. But I have far more important things to occupy ma mind right now."

Just as Tristan turned away from Alasdair, a scream rent the air. He charged toward the stairs. He'd accepted all he could take. The screams had been coming all morning, and he was sure he was about to lose his mind. A wall of men met him at the base of the steps. All four of his brothers-by-marriage blocked his way, just as they had every time he tried to go to his wife.

Liam sipped his whisky by the fire. He was willing to acknowledge it was far too early to be drinking, and it was already his third cup, but it was the only way he would make it through the day while hearing his daughter in pain. He had been through it five times before with his own wife, and it didn't get any easier. He felt for the poor man. Tristan had maintained control of himself longer than Liam expected, but the Sinclair knew time was growing short. At least one of his sons would come away with bruises and probably a broken nose. He had broken his own brother's nose when his wife labored with Callum. It had only taken that one shattering punch for anyone ever to keep him from his wife again.

"Move out of ma way now, or I will move ye all. I will see ma wife." Tristan hissed through his teeth. He clenched his hands, and his fists were white. A vein bulged in his neck and in his temple. He couldn't take it any longer. He had tried to do what the midwife said and to wait belowstairs, but if he heard her scream one more time, he would commit bloody murder to anyone who stood in his way. He tried to take a few calming breaths, but another scream rang through the keep.

"That's it. I'm done waiting." Tristan swung his right fist into Callum's gut and his left fist into Alexander's jaw. They both staggered, and he tried to push through the space between them. Tavish and Magnus latched on to his arms, so he twisted to kick Tavish in the groin. Tavish released him. He head-butted Magnus, but the giant beast laughed. He charged toward the stairs, and Magnus jumped onto his back. Tristan was too livid and too determined to get to his wife to shake Magnus free. He couldn't take the stairs two and three at a time with the extra weight, but he still climbed to the top. Magnus tried to drag his feet and pull him backwards, but they were too evenly matched in strength. They got to Tristan's chamber door and he stopped.

"Unless ye desire seeing bits of yer wee sister that nay brother should ever witness, I suggest ye let go of me. I am going in." That was just the right thing to make Magnus release him. Magnus laughed and nodded. He turned his back but didn't move. "Just as I figured. Ye want to make sure she's well just as much as I do. I kenned it."

"Aye well, she's ma baby sister, and I have always watched

over her. Ye arenae ma favorite person since ye're the one who did this to her."

"Ye dinna need to remind me. I dinna ken if I can go through this again."

"Ha, I give it a few sennights before ye forget yer words, and ye're pawing her again. I bet the two of ye will rival Mama and Da for number of kids."

"I'll remind ye of that when yer turn comes." Tristan pushed the door open before Magnus denied it and slipped into the room.

"Ma laird! Ye canna be in here now. This isnae a place for a mon." The midwife tried to shoo him away, but he walked determinedly to the side of the bed. His wife lay there sweating and pale. Her eyes were closed, and he didn't see her chest rise.

"Mairghread!" Tristan snatched her hand and was ready to shake her when her eyes snapped open.

"I ken ye're here. I could hear ye and Magnus coming up the stairs and then everything ye two said. Ye're nae exactly quiet. I was resting." Mairghread focused on Tristan and observed the sheer terror on her braw husband's face. She squeezed his hand and pulled him toward her. "Help me sit up, Tris—"

Mairghread couldn't finish before another pain tore through her, and she screamed. Tristan was certain he would be sick. He had seen more blood and broken bodies in battle than any one man should, but the sound of his tiny, fierce wife in pain almost broke him. He sank to his knees beside the bed and rested his hands on her shoulders as she leaned against him. She settled back against the pillows and closed her eyes again. Tristan looked around, not knowing what to do with himself or how to help. He felt completely and utterly useless for the first time since he had assumed the duties of laird. He started to stand and release her when he spotted a chair near the bed.

"Dinna ye dare leave me now. I've been waiting for ye for hours and asking for ye." Mairghread didn't open her eyes, but she yanked on his arm. In turn, he glared at the midwife, who'd kept him from knowing his wife wanted him there.

"I amnae going anywhere. I will stay with ye for as long as ye like." Tristan pulled her shoulders forwards and shoved the pillows out of the way.

"Tristan? I need those." Before Mairghread understood why he moved them, he crawled onto the bed and sat behind her. His leg braced her sides, and his chest supported her back.

"I told ye, I amnae going anywhere."

Mairghread breathed a sigh of relief. She was finally comfortable after hours of pain. She pulled his arms around her and rested his hands on her rounded stomach. She placed her hands on top of his. She breathed his scent that never ceased to calm her when upset or arouse her when she was ready to play.

"I love ye, *mo ghaol*." Tristan murmured by her ear. He brushed her sweaty hair from her forehead and put his hand back on her belly. Her belly tightened under it, and it amazed him how hard it had become. He felt her tense as the pain resumed.

"Push, ma lady. Push. It's time. I can see yer bairn's head. A dark head of hair, I can see."

Tristan took hold of Mairghread's hands, and she squeezed with a strength he never imagined a woman would possess. She bore down as hard as she could.

"That's it, ma lady. This one will come out fast now that yer body is ready." The midwife was right. It only took three more tremendous pushes, and their son was out.

"It's a lad, ma laird." The midwife held up the squalling babe for them to both see. He had a head of dark hair, just like his father. The midwife cleaned him, and another woman stepped forward. Tristan hadn't noticed the others in the room until now. There were a few serving women, and a woman he recognized from the village. Mairghread reached out, too exhausted to open her eyes after her initial view of the babe.

"Ma lady, the bairn will be hungry. He needs to eat right away. Then ye can hold him." The midwife turned away. Mairghread lurched upright and tried to climb out of bed.

"Give. Me. Ma. Bairn. Now!"

Tristan tried to pull Mairghread back into bed, but she swung at him. It shocked him that she had any energy left in her body or that she would try to hit him.

The village woman stepped forward and tried to take the baby from the midwife. "Ma lady, I'm yer wet nurse. Noblewomen dinna suckle their own bairns. It just tis nae done."

Tristan's head snapped up when he recognized the voice. He hadn't seen Mary in ages, but she was a woman who he'd been intimate with for an extended period. He wondered how she was a wet nurse if she hadn't birthed her own children. Or had she? When had that happened? Mary hesitated and looked with longing at both him and the bairn.

"He is mine. I willna allow any other woman to nurse him. Give me ma bairn." Mairghread was bordering on hysterical. She hadn't missed the looks from Mary and growled. "I ken exactly who ye are. I ken ye're one of the village wet nurses. I also ken ma husband used to bed ye. I dinna give a damn who ye may be or what yer good intentions are. I will nurse ma own bairn."

Tristan didn't know what to be most shocked about: the fact she knew this woman used to be his lover, a lover he barely recognized, or that she was ready to come to blows over their bairn who was less than five minutes old.

"Mary, give the bairn to Lady Mackay. She made her intentions vera clear. Yer services are appreciated but unneeded."

Once the bairn was in Mairghread's arms, she settled back on to the bed. She had overcome her jealousy despite her ever-expanding waistline during pregnancy. She was aware of who the women from Tristan's past were, but he never once strayed in his attention or affections. Just the opposite. He was almost inseparable from his wife, but that didn't mean she liked other women eyeing her husband.

"Everyone out," Tristan demanded.

"But ma laird, we need to bathe yer wife, and the bedding needs to be changed," the midwife said.

"I ken how to care for ma wife." Mairghread felt the power of his love and devotion in those words, and with that, everyone cleared out of the room. Over the next ten minutes, Tristan set to changing all the bedding, bathing Mairghread, and changing her gown. Through it all, Mairghread cooed at the bairn and nursed. She watched her husband, a braw warrior and laird, do the duties of a chambermaid and lady's maid. She had never felt more love for the man.

"Tristan, what shall we call him?" Mairghread asked as he carried them both back to bed.

"I dinna ken. What would ye like?"

"Liam for his given name, after ma da, and Brodie, after yer da. What think ye?

"Perfect, ma highland lass." Tristan wrapped his wife and child in his arms, and they all fell asleep.

Hours later, Liam looked in on his daughter and her family. His heart pounded with love and pride for the family he and his wife created. He wondered which of his children would be next to start a family and hopefully find love along the way.

THANK YOU FOR READING HIS
HIGHLAND LASS

Celeste Barclay, a nom de plume, lives near the Southern California coast with her husband and sons. Growing up in the Midwest, Celeste enjoyed spending as much time in and on the water as she could. Now she lives near the beach. She's an avid swimmer, a hopeful future surfer, and a former rower. When she's not writing, she's working or being a mom.

Visit Celeste's website, www.celestebarclay.com, for regular updates on works in progress, new releases, and her blog where she features posts about her experiences as an author and recommendations of her favorite reads.

Are you an author who would like to guest blog or be featured in her recommendations? Visit her website for an opportunity to share your insights and experiences.

Have you read *Their Highland Beginning, The Clan Sinclair*

Prequel? Learn how the saga begins! This FREE novella is available to all new subscribers to Celeste's monthly newsletter. Subscribe on her website.

www.celestebarclay.com

Join the fun and get exclusive insider giveaways, sneak peeks, and new release announcements in

Celeste Barclay's Facebook Ladies of Yore Group

THE CLAN SINCLAIR

His Highland Lass **BOOK 1**
His Bonnie Highland Temptation **BOOK 2**
His Highland Prize **BOOK 3**
His Highland Pledge **BOOK 4**
His Highland Surprise **BOOK 5**
Their Highland Beginning **BOOK 6**

THE HIGHLAND LADIES

A Spinster at the Highland Court
BOOK 1 SNEAK PEEK

Elizabeth Fraser looked around the royal chapel within Stirling Castle. The ornate candlestick holders on the altar glistened and reflected the light from the ones in the wall sconces as the priest intoned the holy prayers of the Advent season. Elizabeth kept her head bowed as though in prayer, but her green eyes swept the congregation. She watched the other ladies-in-waiting, many of whom were doing the same thing. She caught the eye of Allyson Elliott. Elizabeth raised one eyebrow as Allyson's lips twitched. Both women had been there enough times to accept they'd be kneeling for at least the next hour as the Latin service carried on. Elizabeth understood the Mass thanks to her cousin Deirdre Fraser, or rather now Deirdre Sinclair. Elizabeth's mind flashed to the recent struggle her cousin faced as she reunited with her husband Magnus after a seven-year separation. Her aunt and uncle's choice to keep Deirdre hidden from her husband simply because they didn't think the Sinclairs were an advantageous enough match, and the resulting scandal, still humiliated the other Fraser clan members at court. She admired Deirdre's husband Magnus's pledge to remain faithful despite not knowing if he'd ever see Deirdre again.

Elizabeth suddenly snapped her attention; while everyone else intoned the twelfth—or was it thirteenth—amen of the Mass, the hairs on the back of her neck stood up. She had the strongest feeling that someone was watching her. Her eyes scanned to her right, where her parents sat further down the pew. Her mother and father had their heads bowed and eyes closed. While she was convinced her mother was in devout prayer, she wondered if her father had fallen asleep during the Mass. Again. With nothing seeming out of the ordinary and no one visibly paying attention to her, her eyes swung to the left. She took in the king and queen as they kneeled together at their prie-dieu. The queen's lips moved as she recited the liturgy in silence. The king was as still as a statue. Years of leading warriors showed, both in his stature and his ability to control his body into absolute stillness. Elizabeth peered past the royal couple and found herself looking into the astute hazel eyes of Edward Bruce, Lord of Badenoch and Lochaber. His gaze gave her the sense that he peered into her thoughts, as though he were assessing her. She tried to keep her face neutral as heat surged up her neck. She prayed her face didn't redden as much as her neck must have, but at a twenty-one, she still hadn't mastered how to control her blushing. Her nape burned like it was on fire. She canted her head slightly before looking up at the crucifix hanging over the altar. She closed her eyes and tried to invoke the image of the Lord that usually centered her when her mind wandered during Mass.

Elizabeth sensed Edward's gaze remained on her. She didn't understand how she was so sure that he was looking at her. She didn't have any special gifts of perception or sight, but her intuition screamed that he was still looking.

A Spy at the Highland Court **BOOK 2**

A Wallflower at the Highland Court **BOOK 3**

A Rogue at the Highland Court **BOOK 4**

A Rake at the Highland Court **BOOK 5**

An Enemy at the Highland Court **BOOK 6**

A Saint at the Highland Court **BOOK 7**

A Beauty at the Highland Court **BOOK 8**

A Sinner at the Highland Court **BOOK 9**

A Hellion at the Highland Court **BOOK 10**

An Angel at the Highland Court **BOOK 11**

A Harlot at the Highland Court **BOOK 12**

A Friend at the Highland Court **BOOK 13**

An Outsider at the Highland Court **BOOK 14**

A Devil at the Highland Court **BOOK 15**

PIRATES OF THE ISLES

The Blond Devil of the Sea **BOOK 1 SNEAK PEEK**

Caragh lifted her torch into the air as she made her way down the precarious Cornish cliffside. She made out the hulking shape of a ship, but the dead of night made it impossible to see who was there. She and the fishermen of Bedruthan Steps weren't expecting any shipments that night. But her younger brother Eddie, who stood watch at the entrance to their hiding place, had spotted the ship and signaled up to the village watchman, who alerted Caragh.

As her boot slid along the dirt and sand, she cursed having to carry the torch and wished she could have sunlight to guide her. She knew these cliffs well, and it was for that reason it was better that she moved slowly than stop moving once and for all. Caragh feared the light from her torch would carry out to the boat. Despite her efforts to keep the flame small, the solitary light would be a beacon.

When Caragh came to the final twist in the path before the sand, she snuffed out her torch and started to run to the cave where the main source of the village's income lay in hiding. She heard movement along the trail above her head and knew the local fishermen would soon join her on the beach. These men, both young and old, were strong from days spent pulling in the full trawling nets and hoisting the larger catches onto their boats. However, these men weren't well-trained swordsmen, and the fear of pirate raids was ever-present. Caragh feared that was who the villagers would face that night.

The Dark Heart of the Sea **BOOK 2**
The Red Drifter of the Sea **BOOK3**
The Scarlet Blade of the Sea **BOOK 4**

VIKING GLORY

Leif **BOOK 1 SNEAK PEEK**

Leif looked around his chambers within his father's longhouse and breathed a sigh of relief. He noticed the large fur rugs spread throughout the chamber. His two favorites placed strategically before the fire and the bedside he preferred. He looked at his shield that hung on the wall near the door in a symbolic position but waiting at the ready. The chests that held his clothes and some of his finer acquisitions from voyages near and far sat beside his bed and along the far wall. And in the center was his most favorite possession. His oversized bed was one of the few that could accommodate his long and broad frame. He shook his head at his longing to climb under the pile of furs and on the stuffed mattress that beckoned him. He took in the chair placed before the fire where he longed to sit now with a cup of warm mead. It had been two months since he slept in his own bed, and he looked forward to nothing more than pulling the furs over his head and sleeping until he could no longer ignore his hunger. Alas, he would not be crawling into his bed again for several more hours. A feast awaited him to celebrate his and his crew's return from their latest expedition to explore the isle of Britannia. He bathed and wore fresh clothes, so he had no excuse for lingering other than a bone weariness that set in during the last storm at sea. He was eager to spend time at home no matter how much he loved sailing. Their last expedition had been profitable with several raids of monasteries that yielded jewels and both silver and gold, but he was ready for respite.

Leif left his chambers and knocked on the door next to his. He heard movement on the other side, but it was only moments before his sister, Freya, opened her door. She, too, looked tired but clean. A few pieces of jewelry she confiscated from the holy houses that allegedly swore to a life of poverty and deprivation adorned her trim frame.

"That armband suits you well. It compliments your muscles," Leif smirked and dodged a strike from one of those muscular arms.

Only a year younger than he, his sister was a well-known and feared shield maiden. Her lithe form was strong and agile making her a ferocious and competent opponent to any man. Freya's beauty was stunning, but Leif had taken every opportunity since they were children to tease her about her unusual strength even among the female warriors.

"At least one of us inherited our father's prowess. Such a shame it wasn't you."

Freya **BOOK 2**

Tyra & Bjorn **BOOK 3**

Strian **VIKING GLORY BOOK 4**

Lena & Ivar **VIKING GLORY BOOK 5**

Printed in Great Britain
by Amazon